I0593656

FAE'S ALPHA
FATED MATES OF THE FAE ROYALS,
SUMMER COURT BOOK 3
HELEN WALTON

WALTON HOUSE PUBLISHING

CONTENTS

Foreword   1

Epigraph   3

1. Briana   4

2. Briana   16

3. Sledge   26

4. Briana   36

5. Sledge   52

6. Briana   63

7. Briana   74

8. Sledge   87

9. Sledge   99

10. Briana   110

11. Briana   119

12. Sledge   129

13. Briana   139

14. Briana   151

15. Sledge   162

16. Briana   170

17. Sledge   185

18. Briana   198

19. Briana   211

20. Sledge   226

21. Briana   234

Epilogue   249

Acknowledgments   253

Also By   254

About Author   257

FOREWORD

AUTHOR NOTE

Choosing character names is not always easy, and there are times you pick them to mean something for the character and the story. I've included the pronunciation and meaning of the names, and if you're like me, and like to know and still pronounce the names the way you read them, then welcome to my club.

Niamh pronounced neeve meaning radiance.

Fintan pronounced fin-tan meaning white fire.

Eamon pronounced aim-on meaning keeper of riches.

Maeve pronounced may-veh meaning intoxicating.

Diarmuid pronounced deer-mid meaning without enemy.

Orlaith pronounced or-lah meaning golden princess.

Rian pronounced ree-an means little king.

Briana pronounced bree-a-nah meaning noble.

Aislinn pronounced ash-lin meaning a vision or dream.

Saoirse pronounced seer-sha meaning freedom.

Lorcan pronounced lor-can meaning silent or fierce.

Ciara pronounced kee-ra meaning dark.

Roisin pronounced row-sheen meaning little rose.

Donagh pronounced done-acka meaning brown-haired warrior.

Deirdre pronounced deer-dree meaning broken-hearted.

Malachi pronounced mal-lah-key means messenger of God.

Ailbhe pronounced all-bay meaning white.

Tadhg pronounced tie-guh meaning poet or philosopher.

From the noblest of deeds love grows.

CHAPTER ONE
BRIANA
THE SUMMER COURT

POWER SWIRLED THROUGH THE gormberry fields as my hands coaxed the drying leaves into a renewed vigor. Vibrant green shoots sprung from the branches, a flush of pink highlighting their tender freshness. As I weaved my Fae power through the bushes, purplish-blue berries formed and filled with plump ripeness. I eased my power back. In the field, the green tendrils of magic swirled as though they weren't quite finished. This extra boost to the plants from my powers would see the Fae through with enough of our staple fruit to satisfy their appetites.

I plucked a handful of gormberries, testing the sweetness of the plump fruit. An explosion of deliciousness exploded over my tongue as I made my way back to the palace.

To home.

My toes sunk into the thick loam of the Summer Court. The rich soil gave us an abundance of nature, from tall trees to lush grasses and everything in between. I placed another round berry in my mouth and rolled it around with my tongue. The Summer Court wasn't as bountiful as it once was. The decline in our spring was affecting everything. I'd lost count of the number of times I'd coaxed the flowers to abundance in the atrium housing the spring to have them wither once again.

It seemed our powers couldn't help us. Which was absurd because we were immortal, with the power to influence nature. Except for the Spring, we couldn't make it run like it once had and if it ever stopped running, then we'd no longer be immortal. Eventually we'd die.

I forced back the shudder that wanted to run through my body.

I was stronger than that.

The palace doors opened as though welcoming me back into its heart. A sense of calm filled my body with each step through the grand hallways. As I neared the sitting room, Mother's soft humming reverberated with her Fae powers. Her sweet notes echoed through the spacious room. My sister, Roisin, sat on the intricate rug of woven vines at my feet while I sat on the two-seater sofa. We absorbed the peace Mother's voice weaved into our hearts with her singing. The one moment in time we all shed our fears for the Fae race.

I brushed then braided Roisin's hair around the small claret flowers of her Fae princess crown. Her long locks were a mess of tangles and knots before I'd run the brush through her silvery strands hanging past her shoulders. My sister was hopeless with her hair. I'd despair of how knotted her tresses would become if she let her hair grow to the length of her bottom like mine and Saoirse's hair.

A deep sigh heaved my chest.

I missed my sister Saoirse more than I imagined.

Mother and Father were tight-lipped about her disappearance from the Summer Court. It annoyed me to no end. Saoirse was my younger sister, like Roisin. I should look out for her. I loved her, even when we didn't see eye to eye. Family was important. More now than ever.

If we didn't have each other, what did we have?

My other sister, Aislinn, burst into the room dressed in her form fitting gown, the bodice so dark purple, it could almost be mistaken for black. She paced from one corner of the room to the other. The glowing candles from the chandelier threw shadows across the gilded mirror above the fireplace we no longer used. I watched her pounding steps, sensing her distress. My fingers threaded without thought through Roisin's hair, the braiding of hair an action I could do in my sleep.

Mother's humming grew louder. Aislinn threw her a glare, stomped over to where she was seated on another plush cream two-seater, and placed her hands on her hips.

"Mother, enough of this. Where's Saoirse?" Aislinn asked the question I was too scared to ask.

Mother's humming jolted to a stop. She blinked her long dark lashes over the glistening of unshed tears in her blue eyes.

"Aislinn," I said in warning, remembering the time I'd held Mother's burned body in my arms while she healed in our Spring Baile. That day I'd thought I'd lose her, but I'd lost so much more.

"No, Briana." She slashed her hand my way. "We haven't seen Saoirse for a long time. Aren't you worried about our sister?"

"Aye." I wrapped a crimson ribbon around Roisin's hair and dropped the finished plait. "Of course, I am."

"Then why aren't you doing something to find her?"

I stood in a rush, sending the deep green fabric of my dress to swish and swell like my power. Roisin scooted across the floor and sat at Mother's feet.

"What do you want me to do?" I flung my hands out wide.

Aislinn huffed. "Anything rather than sit here braiding hair and singing songs."

I raked Aislinn with a scathing glare and called a wooden staff into my hand. Aislinn's hands glowed a silver-purple with her power.

"Girls. Enough." Mother clapped her hands and stood. "Bickering amongst yourselves won't find Saoirse. She's fine." Her eyes filled with tears belying her words that Saoirse was fine.

"Yes, Mother," Aislinn and I said at the same time. We were powerful Fae royal princesses, but Mother was the Fae Queen, and her word was our ruling.

"Leave me and Roisin if you intend to carry on this way." She waved her hand at the door.

Aislinn stomped through the room for the door with another loud huff of air. Dia, her anger would get the better of her one day. The Trappers' actions affected us all, but Aislinn's anger seemed unwarranted compared to what I'd suffered at the hands of the Trappers burning us at the stake. Those fatal nights would haunt me with every breath and beat of my heart.

Nothing and no one could ever take away the pain.

I fought back the bile in my throat whenever I thought about The Trappers and the night I lost my mate and child.

"Mother," I said with a croak in my voice. I cleared my throat. "Please tell us where Saoirse is. We need to know she's safe."

Mother sunk to the sofa in her royal blue gown and clutched the armrest with tight fingers.

"Saoirse will be safe."

"How can you know? She's not here in the Summer Court." I rubbed my wrist. "Is she on Earth?"

"I canna say." Mother hung her head, sending the locks of her silver-gold hair over her face. Her strands were a tad darker than the rest of the family.

"What has Father safeguarded now?" I asked.

Mother sighed and stroked the long braid of Roisin's hair.

"Father's only doing what he thinks is right," Roisin said.

"That's the drawback." I switched hands and rubbed my other wrist. "It's what *he* thinks is right."

Mother hummed again and stroked Roisin's hair. Whether soothing herself or Roisin, I wasn't sure. Aislinn was correct. I couldn't sit here and pretend everything was acceptable. Saoirse was on Earth, in a location we had no knowledge of, and who knew if she required our help? If she needed her big sister. I had to find her. Like she found me that horrific night. I strode from the sitting room and into the great marble halls of the palace.

"Aislinn," I called out. "Wait up."

Aislinn skidded to a halt near her bedroom.

"I'll travel to Earth and search for Saoirse."

"You?" She punched the door with her knuckles, sending a loud rap through the halls. "I should be the one to investigate."

"No. I'm the eldest. I shall leave."

"If you want to play the oldest card, then Rian should hunt Earth for Saoirse," she said.

"'Tis essential Rian stay here and keep an eye on Mother and Father. There's something up with them."

"Besides their missing daughter?" She punched the door again. The rap of her knuckles echoed through the hallway.

I stared at my wrists, wishing the sensation of being restrained didn't haunt me when I was anxious. "Father will not be concerned if I disappear for a while. I can't provide him with a Fae heir any longer."

Unbeknownst to everyone, I kept a secret potion in my room that stopped me from having a Fae heat and allowing any chance to fall pregnant. It'd taken a long time to find a witch with the magic to create such a potion. Then there were the rare times we could escape. It was too risky of a secret to share.

Aislinn leaned on the door. "He hopes I'll choose Gair for a mate and give him heirs to the throne."

"You could."

"I despise Mother's and Father's request we choose mates." She kicked the door with her heel.

"If you take your anger out on your door any further, you won't have a door left."

Aislinn huffed a laugh.

"I'll leave now before I change my mind and realize how idiotic it is to search the whole of Earth for one person."

Aislinn shoved off the door. "I'll walk with you to the spring."

We fell into step through the great marble halls. The soft rustle of my dress was the only sound as we made our approach to the atrium. My brothers, sisters, and I were used to sneaking to the spring in the heart of the palace for our secret trips to Earth. It was the only place we could breach the lock Father placed on the Veil separating our worlds. We stepped inside the atrium with its richness of greenery and flowers. Lorcan was kneeling by the Spring Baile, our spring of life. He lifted his head at our arrival. Blood poured from his nose to splatter the boulder under his knees.

"Lorcan, what happened?" I rushed to my brother's side and tilted his chin to examine his face with a gentle finger.

"Father and I were sparring, and I mentioned Saoirse." He shrugged. "The broken nose was worth being certain she's on Earth with her mate."

"Saoirse has a mate?" I scooped up a handful of water and slapped it to his nose.

With the large handful of our powerful healing water, his nose was repaired in an instant.

"Harsh, Briana. Remind me to never come to you for healing." He wiped the remaining water and blood on his sleeve.

I wrinkled my nose. Men could be so crass. "I'm no healer."

"I'm heading to Earth to find Saoirse," he said.

"No, I'll go." I placed a restraining hand on his arm.

"You?" His eyebrows rose.

"Is that so hard to believe? She's my sister, too."

"Yeah, but you and Saoirse don't always get along."

I rubbed my wrist again. "She should be able to find the cause of the decline to the spring."

"Briana, you can't lump it all on her." He sighed. "This is all our problem. We all need to find a way to remedy it."

"Saoirse has to be the key with her power over water."

Aislinn kicked a stone. "Shite, Briana, maybe you shouldn't go. Perhaps Saoirse left because of you, and you'll make it worse."

"You test my restraint to teach you who is the eldest with my staff," I said, separating the veil into a shimmering silver green. "I love you both too, and I'll find our sister."

Before they could say anything further, I stepped through the veil. Dia, brothers and sisters were annoying. Hundreds of years living with them in the palace grated on my nerves. That and the lowering birth rate of the Fae. The number of babies I'd conceived yet lost before I'd even mentioned their conception to my sexual partner was a heavy burden on my heart. I'd protected Saoirse from her greatest fear of the pain of losing babies by helping her escape to Earth while she was in heat. I was a good big sister. Not a terrible one like Aislinn and Lorcan made me out to be.

Saoirse realized that, didn't she?

I parted the veil onto Earth and stepped through the shimmering silver-green haze. As usual, my departure was through a tree in a forest because of my power's affinity with nature. Except for this time, the forest wasn't empty. Before the tree I stepped from, stood a man. A big, hulking man with a mass of muscle pulling his white t-shirt tight across his chest and bulging biceps. His gaze dropped from his hands which were grasping something over his head, to my face.

His crystal blue eyes widened. "Holy bat balls, where did you come from?"

His voice was low and rich. The husky timbre sent my breathing into short pants. I blinked. This man's voice held a thrall over me. Each moment in his presence sent a hum through my powers. Deep inside energy weaved its way through my heart, twined with the blood pounding through my veins to set my skin tingling.

A creature scrabbled against the tree overhead. Our gazes swung to the branch above. A solid mass of gray fur wriggled in the man's outstretched hands. The animal gained purchase on the tree trunk with its large black claws. He let go, and it climbed the tree to the higher limbs above our heads.

"What is that animal?" I asked, trying to clear the influence this man's presence had on every part of my body.

Our gazes met. His face was inches from mine. A dark, not quite beard lay on his smooth cheeks and surrounded his deep blush lips. His lips called to mine with a force that I struggled to contain.

"Koala," he said, placing his hands on either side of my head on the tree trunk.

I pressed my palms into the smooth bark of the tree behind me, ready to slip back through the veil. He wouldn't be able to follow my departure into the Summer Court. Only Fae could venture into our home. Or a Fae marked mate.

"Koala?" I said with a huskiness that surprised me. "Yes, I've heard of them."

The magnificent man cocked his head to the side, ruffling his spiky black hair with the motion. He studied me, but the action gave me the impression of a man about to kiss me. My lips parted instead of firming into a hard line. His intense gaze dropped to my mouth.

With a deep draw of air, he inhaled, making his already enormous chest expand even further. Another inch and our chests would brush. My nipples hardened as the thought swirled through my mind.

His eyes grew hooded with lust. My body betrayed my struggle against his allure. I shifted closer to him. Drawn to him as much as he seemed drawn to me. He lowered his head and ran his nose over my cheek, into the sensitive skin below my ear, and under my hair. My skin broke out in tiny shivers of delight. He inhaled again. A rumbling growl rippled from his chest. The sound was so sensual that my insides clenched in desire.

He lifted his head and slanted his mouth toward mine. Dia, I desired his kiss. More than I desired to escape back to the Summer Court. One kiss with this heady man. What harm would there be?

His lips brushed the corner of my mouth. A shock of power zapped my lips. My head slammed back into the tree.

"Sorry," he said. "I shouldn't have kissed you, but I couldn't help myself."

My eyes widened. *No. Not possible.* He couldn't be my fated mate. The one destined to call to my powers as well as the woman in me. I brandished my already glowing hands. My power over plants drew the branches of a nearby bush to bend to my will and wrap around the man's lower legs.

"What the?" His gaze dropped to his feet.

I gestured my hands up, and the tree's branches slithered around his wrists and pinned him to the tree.

"I can't," I whispered and ducked out from under his arms.

"Wait," he said.

His voice sent a shiver through my body. I paused and studied the man now tied to a tree. The image excited me more than it should have, but if he was my fated mate, my reaction to him was explainable. Still, my heart wouldn't survive being mated again. I backed up a step.

"Don't go." He tugged on the branches holding him in place. They creaked but held.

"I have to." My gaze flicked to the forest. I couldn't return to the Summer Court without Saoirse. Aislinn and Lorcan would be too smug if I failed to fetch her home. "I have to find my sister."

Dia, why did I tell him that?

"I can help you." He wrenched his thick thighs and tugged on the limbs holding his ankles in place.

"No." I spun and raced into the forest. My powers had transported me to this place on Earth for a reason, and I'd centered my thoughts on Saoirse. She must be nearby. This man couldn't be the purpose I was in this location. He couldn't be the reason my heart pounded for the first time in centuries, or the cause of my body exploding into awareness. Nor the thrumming of my powers.

Even if he was, I couldn't go through the heartache of losing a mate again.

CHAPTER TWO
BRIANA
AUSTRALIA

I SPRINTED THROUGH THE forest, bare feet thumping on the soil beneath the length of my dress, sending a spray of dirt particles up around my ankles. The leaves and twigs of the low-hanging branches snagged on the full skirt of my dress, but I kept darting between trees. The steady pounding of chasing steps resonated behind me. How the man escaped the branches, I'd never understand. My power and the strength of the timber should have held him captive more than long enough for me to flee. I wasn't afraid of him. He was muscular in appearance, but my power was greater. What I needed was time to settle the desire he'd stroked inside me. To repress the lure of my fated mate.

A howl reverberated through the trees. Shite, now animals were chasing me too, along with the indomitable man. I flung aside a large branch with my power and kept dashing through the forest, even though a part of me wished to return to the man and the senses he'd stirred. My blood heated with memories, regrets, pain, and above them all, the allure of the man chasing me.

All I wanted was to find my sister and take her home where she belonged. Perhaps Father was justified in keeping us Fae locked away in the Summer Court. Earth possessed too many variables. Humans were not welcoming of the Fae.

I burst through the trees and skidded across the sandy shore of a lake. Blue water shone for as far as I could see. I had nowhere left to flee ahead of me, and to the sides was more of the abundant forest. Ripples in the water caught my attention. Two heads bobbed in the water. A man rushed toward me while a woman swam slower in my direction. A familiarity in her actions made me peer closer at the woman.

"Saoirse," I said.

"Brianna." She waved both hands in the air.

I let out a breath of relief. Saoirse was safe on Earth. I didn't realize until this moment how concerned I was about her.

Wood snapped behind me.

I spun. At the sight of my sister, I'd momentarily forgotten the man in pursuit.

Except, a large black wolf rushed through the forest and onto the shore of the lake. I staggered back a step and raised my hands, my power was at the ready. The wolf rumbled. I wielded my hands and branches lunged for the wolf's legs. The black beast vaulted to the side and avoided them. The wolf stalked closer. I stepped back. The wolf curled his lips but didn't growl.

A blur of golden fur flew past me and hit the black wolf. The two wolves rolled on the shore of the lake, yipping and growling. I kept my gaze on them and stepped back until my feet hit the cool water of the lake. They stopped their fighting and faced off, the golden wolf standing between me and the black wolf. The black wolf's blue eyes never left mine. A shiver traveled from my toes up to the top of my head.

"I see you've met Sledge," Saoirse said, emerging from the lake and standing beside me.

I dared not take my gaze off the black wolf. "Who?"

"The black wolf, his name is Sledge. He won't hurt you. He's a good friend of mine and Arrow's." Saoirse slipped a wet arm around my waist and said in a loud voice. "You won't hurt my sister, Briana, will you, Sledge?"

The black wolf tilted its head and studied me. A familiar action to the man in the forest. My breath caught in my lungs.

"Arrow is my mate," Saoirse said.

The golden wolf turned his head and almost smiled at Saoirse with a twitch of his gums to reveal pointed white teeth.

I gasped. "Wolf shifters?"

Saoirse laughed. "You're quicker than me. I didn't realize what they were until after Arrow impregnated me."

I faced my sister. She glowed with happiness from head to foot, dressed in a wet pair of pink shorts and a matching top. A huge smile on her face, love in her eyes, and a round bump protruding from her stomach.

"Dia, Saoirse," I whispered and fell to my knees. Tears welled in my eyes.

Saoirse kneeled on the sandy soil with me and wrapped her arms around my shoulders. I cried into her embrace, shedding tears for her happiness. Saoirse had wanted a baby for so long, but she'd been too afraid to conceive one in case the pregnancy ended too. I also wept for the fact I didn't realize my sister had mated and was pregnant, and I wasn't there to help her. I was here now though, and I'd make sure she and the baby were safe.

"Shh." Saoirse patted my back. "Why are you crying?"

I raised my head and scrubbed my cheeks. "I should have been here for you."

"You're here now," Saoirse said.

"Aye." I glanced at her rounded stomach. "I'll stay as long as you want me to."

"What about Father?"

"Father doesn't realize I'm here." I brushed the last of my tears from my cheeks.

"He'll miss you in the Summer Court."

"Aye, but he won't care as much about my disappearance as he would our brothers and sisters. You need me."

Her eyes filled with tears. "Aye," she whispered. "I need my family."

We embraced, with her rounded stomach bulging between us and the dampness of her swimsuit pressing into my dress. The baby kicked. I shifted back at the unexpected force coming from the wee tot.

"Your baby is strong."

She grabbed my hand and placed it on her stomach. "Aye, he is."

"You're not worried?"

Saoirse flicked her gaze to the golden wolf. "On occasion, but my mate reassures me all the time."

I studied the two wolves sitting on the edge of the forest, watching us. Their standoff appeared to have ended.

"A wolf shifter." I shook my head.

"Aye, Father didn't understand our mating." Saoirse hung her head.

The golden wolf stalked to Saoirse and stroked his head against hers. She petted his thick fur in a loving caress.

"Thank you, Arrow, my love."

Wolf Arrow whined.

"Let us head to our house," she said. "Arrow doesn't want to shift and be naked in your presence."

I flicked my hair. "I'd much prefer not to see your mate naked, too."

Saoirse grinned. "You do not appreciate what you're missing out on, then."

"I saw enough when he strode from the lake."

"True, but what's below the surface is so much better."

I snickered. "Does your mate appreciate this side of you?"

"Arrow appreciates all of me." She patted her stomach. "Including this giant ball of a stomach."

"You look beautiful." I helped Saoirse to her feet and threaded my arm with hers. "How far to your house?"

"Not far. A short walk through the forest."

The golden wolf padded ahead of us to a small dirt track through the trees. Saoirse urged me forward to follow. I flicked a glance at the black wolf.

"Sledge will watch our back."

"Hmm." I eyed him with wariness. Would the wolf shifter say anything about our almost kiss? Would he try to kiss me again? The notion made my body hum in delight. I switched my thinking. "Are you worried about being on Earth?"

Saoirse brushed her hair from her face. "'Tis difficult not to worry after." She swallowed. "You know."

I sighed. "Aye."

We fell into an uncomfortable silence. My thoughts flitted back to the time of fire and death, screams and burning flesh. The night I lost my most treasured family. Saoirse's arm tightened around mine like she understood where my mind wandered. Sister solidarity. Her love flowed through her embrace. The love I may not have always shown her. I'd make up for it.

Gulping back the lump in my throat, I said, "I'm sorry if I put pressure on you with the decline in the Spring Baile."

"We've all felt the gravity of the situation."

"I never meant to push you away to Earth."

"You never pushed me away. I found my mate. I discovered what it means to be truly happy." She smiled.

We parted more branches, passed by more trees and reached a cabin nestled in the forest like a piece of nature. It appeared as wild as the wolf strutting onto the porch.

"Come inside." Saoirse opened the timber front door.

Arrow slipped through the open door and padded down a hallway. I stepped inside and took a sweeping glance around the sitting room. Saoirse tugged me to the low navy-blue sofa setting, sat crossed legged and faced me.

The black wolf ventured through the open door.

"Come in, Sledge. You may as well go change, too." Saoirse gestured her hand to the hallway.

Wolf Sledge strutted into the hallway Arrow had disappeared down. His thick, bushy tail swished as he, too, left my sight.

"Does Sledge live here?"

"No," Saoirse said. "Wolf shifters keep clothes stashed around the town."

"This is a wolf shifter town?" My eyebrows rose. How hadn't I sensed that?

"Aye." Saoirse touched my hand. "How's home and the family?"

I slumped back on the soft sofa. "Mother and Roisin are their usual peacekeeping selves. Aislinn is intent on releasing her anger on anything. Rian is missing more and more these days. Ciara has her head buried in books at the library. Lorcan." I shook my head. "And Father." I rubbed my wrist and dropped her intense gaze.

"Nothing has changed then."

"No. If anything, since you disappeared, the family is tenser."

Saoirse slumped back on the couch with me. "I'd hoped the news of my pregnancy would give you joy."

"I didn't hear of your pregnancy."

"You didn't?" She gasped.

"I knew nothing until I saw you."

She flicked her damp hair over her shoulder. "My fault. I made Ciara promise not to tell any of you."

"Ciara knew?" Why did my younger sister know, and I didn't? Did Saoirse think so little of me I wouldn't be ecstatic at her news?

"She followed me to the prison when Father placed me there. I confessed everything to Ciara then."

"You were in prison?" I leaped up from the sofa. What was Father thinking putting Saoirse in prison? What was Ciara thinking, not telling any of us? My younger sister should never have kept these events to herself, but at least Saoirse didn't keep her exciting news from me on purpose.

Saoirse patted the sofa cushion beside her. "Come sit with me and I'll tell you what happened."

I settled back on the sofa. Saoirse divulged the story of her and Arrow, her heat, her pregnancy, and how she saved the wolf pack from a wildfire, Father's ire at her use of powers on Earth, discovering she'd mated to a wolf, how Father imprisoned her because he still wanted to keep her safe in the Summer Court. Then their fight with swords for her freedom, and her gruesome win.

When she finished, I wheezed out a shocked breath. I'd been blind to my sister's ordeal. Too lost in the pain of the past and the concerns for the future of all Fae.

"I'm a terrible big sister." Aislinn and Lorcan were correct. I grabbed Saoirse's hands and squeezed them tenderly. "Can you forgive me for not being there for you?"

Saoirse's bottom lip trembled but she nodded.

"Tell me about your mate."

"Arrow." She sighed. "He's amazing."

"I can see you love him."

"Very much."

"I remember wolf shifters from our earlier times on Earth. They are intense and protective creatures."

"Aye, Arrow possesses all those qualities and more. He can cook."

I raised my eyebrows.

"And I'm eating a lot at present." She placed her hand on her stomach.

"I remember the hunger." I tapped my chest. The pain of losing a child would never go away.

"Lorcan said you entertained Tadgh in my place. You didn't conceive, did you?"

"No. I haven't experienced a heat in over a century." I glanced away. It wasn't a total lie. I'd drunk the potion before my heat begun but she didn't know that.

"Good, I wouldn't want to cause more pain for you."

"I make my own choices." I fidgeted on the sofa. "Right now, I'm choosing to stay on Earth and help you until the baby is born. You'll need a Fae to oversee the birthing process."

The air left Saoirse's lungs in a loud puff. "Thank you. I'm nervous about the birth."

"It'll be fine. Painful. But that's normal."

I smiled and patted her hand. I wouldn't tell her how painful giving birth was. It was an experience no one could prepare you for. The contractions squeezing your body so hard you believed your body was about to split in two. As much as I loved my sister, I wouldn't add to Saoirse's fears about the birth.

"Normal?" She squinted her eyes at me.

"Aye. Your body will recognize what to do when the wee tot is ready to enter the world."

A wistfulness passed through me I'd never experience that again.

She caressed her stomach. "Arrow assures me if I were to give birth now, he'd survive like human babies do at this time."

"Your mate sounds smart and perfect for you."

Saoirse batted her lashes while a smile tugged her lips. "So, why was Sledge chasing you through the forest?"

CHAPTER THREE
SLEDGE

I YANKED ON THE pair of my gray tracksuit pants and white t-shirt in Arrow's and Saoirse's spare bedroom. It was their house now they were mated. I was happy for my best friend and his happiness with Saoirse gave me hope I'd one day have it myself with a mate. Arrow swung open the door and shut it behind him. A thick pink robe hung over his arm. Saoirse and her love of pink and Arrow's love of pleasing her. Would I do small things like him to please my mate?

The closed door wouldn't stop Saoirse's and her sister, Briana's, voices from reaching us with our wolf hearing. I'd already overheard enough of their conversation to learn the sisters loved each other, but they underwent problems back home.

Arrow folded his arms over his chest.

"What?" I shoved a pair of sneakers on my feet and tied the laces.

"Care to explain why you were chasing Saoirse's sister through the forest?"

"Dude, don't start." I yanked the shoelace, and it snapped off in my fingers.

Arrow chuckled.

"Shit." I scowled.

"You're so screwed." Arrow grinned.

"I know." I raked a hand through my hair.

"You suspected one of Saoirse's sisters was your mate all along," he accused.

I stood and threw the broken shoelace in the bin by Arrow's feet near the door.

"I did. Saoirse's scent was familiar. Like family."

"Why didn't you tell me?" He stroked his chin.

I stalked to the window. "Tell you what? I wasn't sure."

"And now you are?"

"Yeah." I tapped the window frame and stared unseeing at the forest outside. "I recognize she's my mate."

"Does she understand too? Saoirse didn't realize to begin with."

I shrugged. Her words and her body's reaction to my nearness made me uncertain whether she was unaware I was her mate or opposed to the idea.

"We should go out there and find out then." Arrow opened the bedroom door.

The women's voices drifted to us louder and clearer. I stiffened at the mention of Briana entertaining a Fae named Tadgh. A low growl rumbled from my chest.

Arrow smirked. Damn. My shitty friend enjoyed this too much.

"Dude, keep it together." He slapped my back.

I curled my lip and flashed him my teeth.

"Welcome to the club." Arrow strode from the room.

I muttered under my breath and followed him into the sitting room.

Saoirse's and Briana's heads swung our way. Briana's gaze landed on my chest. Pink tinged her cheeks. Seemed my mate wasn't immune to my looks. It was a start, but then her reaction in the forest left me wondering if she wanted me or not.

Arrow held out the robe for Saoirse. She stood and slipped her arms into the long sleeves and cinched the robe around her growing waist. Arrow nuzzled her neck, tugged her into his arms, and settled on the sofa with Saoirse against his side. They were sickeningly sweet in their affection.

"Arrow, this is my sister, Briana. Briana, this is my mate, Arrow," Saoirse said and nodded at me. "Over there is our friend, Sledge."

"A pleasure to meet you." Briana smiled at Arrow. "Fae don't feel the cold."

Arrow grinned. "Saoirse keeps telling me that, but she lets me wrap her up now it's winter and the temperature has dropped."

"Sledge, sit down, would you?" Saoirse said.

I blew out a breath and sat on the sofa near Briana since Arrow had left no room next to him. Her scent teased my senses. The fresh aroma of plants, and the subtle perfume of a flower. I inhaled. *Which flower did she remind me of?* All of them. I spread my arms along the back of the sofa. My fingers ended up near Briana's shoulder.

Briana's gaze flicked to my face, then my hand. "Donna touch me."

"I wouldn't dream of touching you unless you asked me to, sweetheart." I winked.

She opened her mouth, no doubt to argue I'd already touched her without her asking me to, but her mouth snapped shut. I smiled and winked again. Briana rolled her eyes. Damn, her rolling her eyes at me was sexy as hell.

"I won't be asking." She faced Saoirse and Arrow, giving me her back.

She'd thrown the challenge down to the wolf inside me and given me an unobstructed view of her supple neck. My wolf clawed at my insides, eager to make his mate submit. Intent on marking her. I forced him to stay within. I didn't need another set of ruined clothes today. As it was, I'd have to go back and gather my shredded clothes from the forest when I left here.

"Is Tadgh your man?" I asked, not quite keeping the growl out of my voice. If she loved another, then there would never be anything between us. If she didn't love him, well...

"What?" She spun her head back to me.

"Tadgh's a Fae back in the Summer Court," Saoirse said. "He's no one important to Briana."

"Saoirse," Briana snapped, and glared at her sister.

Saoirse rolled her fluffy covered shoulders under Arrow's arm. Arrow grinned, his lips stretched wide, and his pointed teeth flashed. He silently laughed at me.

"Why were you chasing my sister, Sledge?"

I scraped my nails along the material of the sofa. "We had unfinished business."

Briana swung her glare at me. "We have no business, unfinished or otherwise."

She'd get a sore neck with all her back and forth movements. I'd rub it better for her if she asked.

"I beg to differ. Or do I need to remind you of the way you tied me up with branches and vines?"

Arrow laughed, and Saoirse giggled.

"She plays dirty with her powers," Saoirse said.

"So I found out when we met." I dropped my hands to my knees and placed them palms up. "I was returning a koala to the forest. Next thing I'm tied to a tree. You can't blame a wolf shifter for chasing you down."

Briana flapped her mouth again.

I grinned. She didn't want to tell her sister about our tender almost kiss. Fine by me. I'd use it to my advantage.

"He's right," Arrow said. "Any wolf shifter would've chased you down after that. Lucky for you, it was Sledge you tied to the tree. Others might not have been so restrained in their retribution."

Briana scoffed. "I didn't hurt him. There was no harm in what I did."

"I am owed retribution." I spun my hands and tapped my thighs.

Briana's gaze dropped to my fingers. She swallowed louder than normal.

"What did you have in mind?"

I ran my gaze over her face and settled on her lips. Her breath hitched. Damn, I wanted to kiss her. This time with no gentleness. Why the hell had I said I wouldn't touch her unless she asked? I was a dumbass. More than that, I was a raging wolf raring to bite his mate. I tugged the collar of my t-shirt. The itch to change almost unbearable.

"I'll have to get back to you." I stood before my wolf claimed his mate for himself with no thought to how it would affect me as a man. Wolf shifter females loved the dominant side of male wolves and desired to submit to us, but my mate was Fae. Not a creature I held much knowledge of, but at least Saoirse had acquainted me with her ways. As her sister, Briana would be more like her than a wolf shifter.

Briana's gaze landed on my junk since it was in her face now I stood opposite her. Pink rose to her cheeks, but she didn't drop her gaze. Her sweet scent grew headier.

"I should collect my clothes from the forest before it gets dark."

The blush on Briana's cheeks traveled down her neck in the direction I wanted to follow with my lips. I hoped her delicate blush was from the idea of me being naked. A guy could hope.

"I'll see you tomorrow for sword practice, Saoirse." I stepped to the front door.

Briana's gaze didn't leave my junk. I wanted to laugh at her obsession. All she had to do was ask, and it'd be hers. It was already hers. She just needed to claim me first. My cock twitched. Briana's eyes widened with a surge of desire. I spun around before the twitch grew into more. The tracksuit pants did little to hide my swinging dick.

I tugged the front door open, stripped my clothes, folded them with the neatness instilled by my ma and left them on the swing seat on the porch. Saoirse or Arrow would put them back in the spare bedroom when they found them. Which, if I knew my best friend, would be at sunrise. The guy was way more romantic than me, sitting with his mate watching the sunrise. I'd rather spend the morning in bed with my mate.

Briana's heated gaze on my body left me with a roaring ache. With a flash of fur, I changed into my wolf and raced into the forest. The damn woman had me tied up in knots already, and we hadn't even placed our mating marks on each other yet. My wolf howled at me to go back and mark her as mine. To sink our teeth into her flushed flesh and rub our scent over her body. Inside her body.

Animals scurried out of my way. I didn't blame them. The wolf was on a rampage with the setting of the sun. His thirst for pursuing his mate turned to other creatures he could hunt. He caught a scent and slowed. I sniffed the trail. Feral pig. Those animals were a nuisance to the Australian wildlife. They tore up vegetation, spread weeds, degraded soil, and water, preyed on native animals, and carried diseases. I'd do the countryside a favor by killing one. Plus, a feral pig was far tastier than shop bought pork.

I slunk through the thick bushes, keeping my scent downwind. The eucalyptus trees helped hide my wolf scent from the feral animal. I caught sight of the black pig and froze. The pig raised its head. Enormous tusks jutted from its lower jaw. Its beady eyes scanned the bushes to the left of me. I stayed still, not even breathing. The animal returned to rooting around in the foliage. I puffed in quick breaths and inched forward, one paw at a time. The pig turned its black butt to my face. I curled my upper lip and lunged for the beast. The pig squealed but stood its ground. I circled the beast. It kept its lethal tusks pointed my way.

This was easier with the pack, but I wasn't about to let this feral pig go. Not when my wolf asserted a thirst for letting out his pent-up frustration. I nipped at the pig's face, missing its flesh. It squealed and ran. Big mistake. If it'd stood its ground, it would have held a better chance of survival. Running incited my wolf more. I took the pig down, sinking my teeth into its softer flank. A pig's skin was tough, but this spot gave to the pressure of my teeth. Blood spurted into my mouth. The pig's legs thrashed in the air. I sunk my teeth in harder. The noises from the pig grew louder. I ripped a chunk of flesh from the flank and risked the lethal tusks to sink my teeth into the throat of the animal. I hated to see them suffer in death. A quick death was the least I could do. The boar gave one last thrash of his head, catching my foreleg and sending a sharp pain through my limb. I clamped my teeth harder, and the pig stopped all noise and movement. I held on for a few moments more then let go, and stood puffing for breath over the beast.

When my breathing returned to normal, I laid on the churned soil from our tussle and licked the wound on my leg. The boar's tusks stung. Lucky for me, it was a graze. He could've broken my leg or gored my stomach. *What was I thinking, taking a boar down by myself?* My mate had my mind elsewhere.

I shifted back to human form. The change caused the wound on my arm to drip more blood. I shook my arm, flicking the blood onto the bright green of the leaves in the surrounding bushes. At least the pack would have a feast tomorrow night. I hoisted the feral boar, weighing close to a hundred kilograms, over my shoulder and strode through the forest. On the way back to Crystal Creek, I collected my shredded clothes and checked on the koala I'd released. The small gray animal was high in the tree, nestled between two branches, snoozing. One success story from the wildfires over summer. I had one more koala at home still awaiting release back into the wild.

The day settled into darkness on my trek home. The weight of the boar was a heavy reminder of the differences between me and my mate. After spending time with Saoirse, I grasped they were vegetarians, but Arrow said she understood his need for meat.

Would Briana be as understanding?

There was a haughtiness in her expression whenever she looked at me that told me she'd use it as another excuse to avoid me. But she wouldn't have a chance. I'd overheard her say she'd stay on Earth until Saoirse's baby was born. A few months would be a long enough time for me to win Briana over, because damned if I'd let my mate go without a fight. And a fight would be ahead once my father, the pack Alpha, found out a Fae was my mate. As next in line to the pack Alpha title, he expected me to mate with one of the female wolf shifters he'd fetched over from England in exchange for two of our males. But those women weren't my mate.

Briana was.

CHAPTER FOUR
BRIANA

I THUMPED THE PILLOW on the bed for the umpteenth time. How many times did Saoirse and Arrow have sex in one night? Surely, she required sleep with her pregnancy. I gave up any attempt at sleep in the spare bedroom, slipped out from under the blanket, wriggled into my dress, and tiptoed through the house and to the front door. Shadows flitted amongst the trees in the night, and with them, a pair of pale blue eyes blinked back at me.

Sledge.

How long had he stalked the forest around the house? Since he left? My foolish heart gave a little flip he'd kept watch. Kept us safe. I stepped to the swing seat and sunk onto the soft cushions, except a lump bulged against my left buttock. I tugged the rumpled material from under my bottom and held up the fabric. Sledge's clothes. His masculine woodsy scent drifted from the material. I possessed the unnerving urge to lift them to my nose.

"Did you come back for these?" I flapped the clothes, only making his alluring aroma waft over me.

Sledge slunk out of the bushes in his black as midnight wolf form. He was spectacular as a wolf, I'd give him that. The wolf padded up the stairs. His form wavered, and he changed right before my eyes into a glorious specimen of a man. Muscles upon muscles under smooth skin and a trail of dark hair led downward to where I dare not let my gaze wander. He was magnificent as a man, too. My mouth dried and my bottom lip fell open, letting the cool winter's night air into the heat of my mouth.

Sledge tugged the clothes from my now limp hands and dressed in his tracksuit pants. I couldn't force my gaze away from his naked chest. Not that I wanted to. I was in danger of letting this wolf shifter lure me into liking him, wanting him, into more. He settled onto the swing seat. His body so close sent my body and mind into a tangled confusion. He pushed the chair into motion with his bare feet.

"What are you doing out here, Princess?" Sledge asked.

I groaned. "Arrow and Saoirse..." I gestured my hand toward the house.

Sledge chuckled. "Yeah, they're always going at it."

"They're not quiet either."

"Most aren't when they're having good sex."

"Sex is sex." I stroked my hands down my thighs, needing something to do besides grasping for him.

Sledge leaned forward and peered into my face. "Sweetheart, sex is not sex. There's a whole slew of different types. I figured you'd have more experienced in the sex department since you're older."

Lifting my chin, I met his peering gaze and said, "I have experience."

"Yeah? What sort?"

I stiffened my spine. I wouldn't think of sex with Sledge. "None of your business."

He chuckled, leaned back in the seat, and placed his arm along the back behind my shoulders. Dia, I craved to rest back in his brawny embrace.

"I think the princess protests too much. We're only talking."

"Fine." I huffed. "And stop calling me sweetheart."

Sledge grinned, causing a dark splotch on his face to crack.

I peered closer at his face in the darkness. Darker splotches marked his face everywhere.

"What did you get on your face?" I swiped the mark, but nothing came away. The mark was dry and crusty to my touch.

"A bit of blood, no doubt."

"Whose blood?" I scanned his body, checking for injuries this time instead of lusting after him. My gaze snagged on the bulge of his forearm where a long slash of darkness marred his perfection. I snatched his arm into my hands. "What happened?"

"Don't worry about it." He tugged his arm out of my grip.

I bolted up from the swing seat. My hands glowed with a surge of my power, ready to defend everyone. Even this wolf shifter. "Who was it?"

"Bree, sit down. There's no one out there going to hurt you. I tangled with a feral boar, is all."

My power retreated in a wave of relief. "Daft man." I grabbed his arm and urged him from the seat. "Come inside and let me clean your wound."

"I'll be okay. It's a scratch." He protested but stood.

I poked my finger into the 'scratch'.

"What the fucking bat balls?" He scowled.

"If 'twas a scratch, it wouldn't hurt when I touch it."

"Damn, woman, you're harsh."

"Wait until I'm finished dressing your wound before you complain." I smirked.

I tugged Sledge inside the dark house. He let me despite his declaration his wound was a scratch. We made our way to the bathroom connected to my bedroom. I ignored the rumpled blanket on my bed and flicked on the light switch inside the bathroom, bathing us in a golden glow. Sledge's red, blood-splattered face grinned back at me. He was even more alluring covered in blood, and a gaping wound on his arm. My heart flipped with the contact of my fingers on his arm. I swung my gaze from his amused face to the wound. A deep gash slashed the top of his forearm from wrist to elbow. I eased the edges apart.

"Not so deep as to need stitches."

"Told you it was a scratch."

"Even scratches need attention. Feral boars can cause a lot of damage. Why did you take one on?"

He shrugged his massive shoulders. "I needed to let out a bit of energy."

I huffed. "Men."

Sledge chuckled. The sound echoed off the bathroom tiles. I turned on the taps and forced his arm under the running water. He sucked in a breath. I washed the dirt and blood from his so-called scratch.

"Take it easy, would you?" He grumbled.

I turned off the water and dabbed the still oozing wound with a towel, then rummaged in the bathroom drawers for a bandage. I found a drawer stacked with all manner of first aid care. A smirk stretched my lips, as I unscrewed a bottle of antiseptic liquid and poured it on his wound.

Sledge yanked his arm from my hand.

"Woman." He growled.

"'Tis a little scratch, is it not?" I held up the bandage.

He thrust his arm into my space, almost grazing my breast with his fingertips. I wrapped the white bandage around his arm, ignoring the way my nipples tightened from his nearness. I should have insisted he shower too, with the dirt and blood covering his face and upper body. It made me quiver inside to imagine him naked under the water, washing himself. This man wouldn't be afraid to rip out hearts to protect those he loved. *Who did he love?* I knew nothing about him. I didn't want to appreciate anything about him. If I did, he'd be even harder to resist.

"There." I slapped tape on the end of the bandage over his scratch.

Sledge held his arm. "You are the worst nurse ever."

"Thank you." I smiled.

Sledge's lips spread into a heated smile. He inched closer.

"You like a bit of pain, don't you?" he asked.

Our breaths mingled. Fiery. Intense. I dragged his aroma into my lungs with each inhale. He slanted his head, hovering his mouth over my lips. So close, like the first time in the forest. I longed to experience the tingle of rightness his lips generated on mine.

"I—" I licked my lips.

"Bree, ask me." He breathed against me.

I blinked sluggishly, and said in a husky voice, "Ask you what?"

"Ask me to touch you. To kiss you."

I shifted back until my back hit the cool tiles of the wall. He followed me and placed his hands on either side of my head but didn't touch me. All night he hadn't touched me, but I'd touched him.

"No," I whispered, my heart flipping inside my chest.

"Okay," he murmured. His gaze roamed over my face.

"Okay?" I swallowed. I'd expected him to push me. To take what sizzled between us. What fate meant us to be.

"Yeah. You'll ask me one day. I can wait for you."

He shoved off the wall and opened the bathroom door.

My stomach roiled at the thought he would leave. I almost told him to stay, but I couldn't give him hope I'd one day ask him for everything.

"Thanks for playing nurse." He peered over his shoulder with a sultry smile. "Next time, how about you wear a little nurse's costume?"

With his smarmy line, my anxiety settled. I picked up the damp towel and hurled it at him. It fell at his feet. He disappeared down the dark hallway. The front door creaked open and closed. I sagged against the wall and slid down until my bottom landed on the white floor tiles. I placed my head on my raised knees. Dia, the wolf shifter stirred things in me long forgotten.

Emotions and feelings I didn't have a right to feel ever again.

For if I couldn't protect my first mate, how would I protect another?

Saoirse and Arrow were up at the crack of dawn. How they coped on so little sleep was beyond me. After the night I had, my eyes were bleary, my mood despondent. Heaviness sat in my heart. I'd promised Saoirse I'd stay with her until the baby was born, but with Sledge, and what he was, well ... shite.

Sledge arrived at the house looking more attractive than ever, dressed in a black t-shirt, skintight black pants, and carrying a sword. My eyes bugged out of my head. Those pants left naught to my imagination.

"I know." Saoirse nudged my shoulder. "When I first met Sledge, I assumed his muscular build meant he had a little penis."

I choked on a laugh. "It's anything but little."

"Surprising, right? Imagine what it's like erect?"

My cheeks heated. I didn't need to imagine. My mind was already there picturing him hard while he watched me play a nurse in a costume. The blood in my body heated into an inferno. I sat with a loud clunk on the porch steps. Which was worse. It brought me eye level with the penis we'd been discussing as Sledge walked toward us from his truck.

"Good morning, princesses."

"Morning, Sledge," Saoirse padded down the stairs. "Ready to get your ass handed to you again?"

"Always when it's from a pretty girl."

Saoirse laughed, but my power flowed to my hands in a fit of unwarranted jealousy. Saoirse and Sledge stared at me.

"Briana, what's wrong?" Saoirse asked.

"Nothing," I snapped.

Arrow strode through the front door clad in a navy-blue uniform and swooped Saoirse into his arms, saving me from further questions. They kissed with the heat of a thousand suns. I twisted from the sight, but my gaze ended up on Sledge, who smiled at me with a too-knowing smile.

"I'm off to work. Take care of my mate, Sledge," Arrow said.

"Always." Sledge unsheathed the sword he'd carried from his pickup.

Arrow shook his head and strode to his pickup truck, rolled down his window, and waved. He revved the truck and sped out of the dirt driveway.

Saoirse brandished her hands and called a water sword to life with her power. The waves in the blade swished with each movement she made. My sister and Sledge squared off in the dirt driveway. Saoirse was exceptional with a sword, Father was the only Fae she couldn't best. There was no chance a wolf shifter would better her, especially since she was pregnant with his friend's child. From what I'd seen Arrow trusted Sledge, so did Saoirse. My stomach did a little flip of unease for a different reason.

"You're sparring here?" I asked. Why was I experiencing a concern for Sledge?

"Sure, why not?" Sledge asked.

"What about your arm?" I pointed to his arm. "Shouldn't you spar on a timber floor?"

"My arm is fine." Sledge shook it in my direction. His skin held a faint pink slash along his forearm, but the wound had healed. "Wolf shifters heal quick."

I pursed my lips. He'd let me be concerned for him and play nurse for no reason last night.

"What are you two talking about?" Saoirse asked, tapping the water sword on the ground.

"A boar scratched my arm last night and Briana tended to it for me."

Saoirse grinned.

"'Twas nothing." I rubbed my wrist.

Saoirse's smile tugged down into a frown.

I let go of my wrist and waved my hand. "Get on with it, then. I want to see you win, Saoirse."

Sledge blew me a kiss.

Of all the...

Their swords met with an earsplitting thud sending birds into flight with a wild flap of wings from the nearby trees.

"Good," Saoirse said and swung at Sledge again.

He blocked her blow and swung at Saoirse. Saoirse blocked with ease and spun around, aiming a low blow at his legs. Sledge sprung back, narrowly missing the sharp water blade of Saoirse's sword. My breath caught in my throat.

"Come on, don't let her get you on the run," I said.

Sledge's gaze swung to me. I rolled my eyes. *What was he thinking, taking his attention off his opponent while sparring?* Saoirse lunged and delivered what would have been a killing blow to his chest, but at the last second, her water blade disintegrated into nothing. I scooted closer to the edge of the stairs, the word no on the tip of my tongue.

"Shit," Sledge said.

I bit back my reaction and pretended I hadn't been about to jump to his rescue.

"Round one to me." Saoirse padded back to the center of the driveway.

He groaned and faced off with Saoirse again. This time, his attention didn't waver. Their swords clashed with a loud clang. They stepped around each other. Tested each other's reach. Sledge had a longer reach, but Father taught Saoirse the distance of a man's arm length in their sparring sessions. *What would Father say about Saoirse sparring while pregnant?* I was a little surprised her mate allowed her to sword fight while carrying his offspring. Saoirse delivered another pretend kill blow to Sledge's neck this time.

I clapped my hands. "Well done."

Saoirse puffed and leaned on her sword. "It's getting difficult to maintain my balance and speed with the baby growing."

I rose from the stairs and massaged her back. "Wait another month and see how hard it is."

Saoirse groaned. "How much bigger will I get?"

"I'm not sure. You're quite large for a Fae, but you're having a part wolf shifter baby."

Sledge chuckled. "Wolf shifters have enormous babies. All the fur and teeth and claws. They rip their way out too."

Saoirse gasped and paled.

I slapped Sledge on the arm. "Stop teasing my sister."

His gaze snagged on my hand, still on his arm. I snatched it away from the warm dampness of his alluring skin. Every time I touched him, a tingle raced through my nerves and tugged at my chest.

"I have to get her back somehow for always beating my ass."

Saoirse brightened and walked to the porch steps where I'd sat watching them spar. "You two can spar now. I might not pull my blade if I went again." She smirked. "After that comment." She fluttered her hand and a water Katana flowed into her grasp.

Sledge held up his hands and stepped back. "Okay, okay. No more teasing about the birth of your tiny wolf."

"Sledge," Saoirse growled.

"You're more like a wolf shifter every day." Sledge turned to me. "What about it, Bree? Want to hand me my ass?"

"Most definitely." I grinned. And what a fine ass he had.

Sledge twirled his sword.

"You can put that away." I clapped my hands and called two staffs with my power.

"Wait, what?"

I grabbed his sword and tossed it to Saoirse, who caught it with ease, then handed him a staff.

"Come. I'll teach you a couple of blocks first." I waggled my fingers until he stepped forward. "Stop there. We need to be this distance away from each other." I held up my staff. "Do the same."

Our staffs crossed in the middle.

"Hold the staff in your right hand and place against the hollow of your right foot. Now bow forward. Good. Turn your head and face your opponent."

Sledge's gaze hit mine with heat and intensity. I held his searing gaze, even though the way he stared at me made me want to blush.

"Kick the staff up into your other hand with your foot. I'll step forward with a swing and you'll block with yours over your head."

Sledge followed my directions, and our staffs slammed together with a loud crack of wood on wood.

"You don't pull your hits," Sledge said.

I grinned. "Again. This time, get ready to block low."

We faced off. I kicked my staff into my hands and swung at Sledge's head. He blocked with simplicity, then I swung at his crotch from below and he blocked with earnest.

"Rock back and hit in the middle with power," I directed.

Our staffs slammed with a bang.

"Now I'll thrust, and you'll block with a horizontal swing."

"You'll thrust, huh? I thought that was my job." Sledge waggled his eyebrows.

Saoirse giggled.

I jabbed at his stomach with the end of my staff. He blocked with a quick swipe of his staff.

"Spin your staff and retreat. I'm coming at you."

Sledge winked. "You can come on me."

The nerve of the man attempting to put me off. I spun my staff in two hands while Sledge twirled his in one hand and backed up. When he couldn't go back any further because the trees were at his back, we swung.

Our staffs clanged in the middle again. I slammed his staff down to the ground, putting Sledge in a vulnerable position.

"Duck," I said and twirled my staff at his neck, aiming to decapitate him if this was an actual fight.

"Jump," I said, swinging at his feet next.

He missed the sweep of my staff by mere millimeters.

"Block your face." I jabbed at his face.

Sledge blocked with a grin. "You out for my blood, sweet thing?"

"No." I twirled my staff.

"You like to win."

I shrugged. "Let's do the set again without my instructions this time." I strode back to the middle of the driveway with my dress swishing about my legs.

Sledge joined me and hoisted his staff. "What do I get if I win?"

"You won't win." I raised my staff.

"But what if I do?" He crossed his staff with mine in the center.

"You won't win, so name anything." I met his penetrating gaze.

"If I win, you let me touch you."

"Deal." I nodded without another thought. He wouldn't beat me even with his attempts to distract me.

"You didn't ask how I'll touch you," he said with a deep huskiness that he may as well have been touching me when he said it.

Heat roared through my body. Dia, his voice filled my soul, and brought my body to life. My gaze lowered to his firm chest, the fit of his t-shirt over his ripped stomach, and lower to the impressive bulge in his pants.

Saoirse clapped her hands. "Begin."

Sledge swung his staff. I blocked just in time. This wasn't how it was meant to go. I ignored my traitorous body's reaction to Sledge and swung my staff at his crotch. Sledge blocked with a laugh.

Our staffs banged in the middle. I jabbed at his stomach, and he blocked with ease even though I put more force into my attack. He was a quick learner. I spun my staff. Sledge spun his and stepped back until his back brushed against the trees. We struck at the same time, our staffs clanging together. I swiped his down to the ground, then swung at his head. He ducked. I swiped low and collected his legs too fast for the wolf shifter to react. Sledge grunted and flew back through the air.

Without thought, my power surged and called a collection of vines to form into a pillow to cushion Sledge's landing.

"Oomph!" He grunted, his heavy body hitting the vines with a crunch.

I dissolved the staffs with my power and held out my hand.

"Guess you won." He clasped my hand.

Everything that fate meant us to be to each other flowed between our palms. My power surged. The vines crept around our hands, linking us together. My body hummed with tension, desire, and a long-buried yearning. Sledge's eyes widened. I wrenched him to his feet and let go.

"Bree." He swayed toward me.

I planted a hand on his chest. "Not happening. Never again."

CHAPTER FIVE

SLEDGE

FUCKING BAT BALLS. MY mate handed my ass to me, then seared me with her touch. I quirked an eyebrow at her quick denial and lies. Lies our fate wouldn't happen. Lies she didn't want it. Scenting lies was my new favorite perk of being a wolf shifter when it emanated from my mate. She experienced the power surging between our palms. Her body flushed with the fragrant scent of arousal whenever she was around me, even more so when her power thrummed from her palms. She wasn't immune to me. Far from it. But she kept denying what was between us.

Briana swiped her hand from my chest and flung the vines back into the forest with her power. She was sensational.

I cleared my throat.

Saoirse walked over to us. "You saved him."

"Aye," Briana said. "He's meant to be protecting you while your mate is away. I couldn't very well injure him."

I cocked an eyebrow.

Saoirse eyed her sister like she'd grown a new head.

Briana rubbed her wrist.

What was it with her wrist? Was there something on it annoying her?

"He'd heal with his shifter power." Saoirse shrugged any concern for my welfare away.

My exceptionally enhanced wolf shifter hearing picked up the reverberations of Arrow's Ford Ranger engine through the quiet forest.

"Arrow will be here soon."

Saoirse grinned. I craved to see Briana smile in the same way for me.

"Have we been at it that long?" Briana asked.

"All day. I can go all night too." I winked at her.

Briana rolled her eyes. I bit back a groan at how such a small thing made me even hotter for her.

Arrow's silver Ranger rolled into view and stopped in the driveway. He strode over to us as we stood near the forest.

"Is everything all right here?" Arrow asked.

"Wonderful." Saoirse flung her arms around his neck. "Briana taught Sledge how to fight with staffs and beat him."

"Yeah?" Arrow's golden eyes flashed with humor.

"Shut up," I groused. "I'd like to see you do better."

"Aye," Saoirse added. "You'd be better than Sledge."

Arrow wrapped his arm around Saoirse's waist and fit her into his side. "Maybe later. I thought you'd be itching to go to the waterfall."

Saoirse brushed her hair over her shoulder. "I am."

"Let's go."

"Wait," I said. "How did the meeting go?"

Arrow slid his hand into Saoirse's. "Good. The Alpha gave the go-ahead for us to train Dean and Jonathon for our team."

"That's good news. Dean and Jonathon are good friends. They might be close to the twins with training."

Saoirse whispered in Arrow's ear.

"We'll be back in a little while," Arrow said. "Unless ... you want to come to."

"No," I said. I knew they enjoyed sex at the waterfall, and I didn't want to be there for that, plus I was certain Briana didn't wish to be there for that either after her complaints last night.

"No," Briana said too as though she'd read my mind.

Arrow and Saoirse disappeared into the forest hand in hand.

"What team?" Briana asked.

"Our firefighting team," I said.

"You're a firefighter?" Briana's face paled.

"Yeah. Are you okay? Do you want to sit down?"

She rubbed her wrist in a furious motion.

I stretched out a hand, then dropped it. "Do you want to tell me about it?"

She flicked her gaze to mine. Fear and pain flashed in the pale blue depths. I'd seen the same expression in many animals' eyes while fighting a wildfire. The look coming from Briana's eyes punched me in the stomach.

"Bree, sweetheart, take a deep breath. Focus on my eyes."

Briana inhaled. Not deep enough.

"Deeper." I breathed deep, filling my lungs with her scent of fresh plants and sweet flowers.

She filled her lungs, her shoulders lifted, and her chest expanded beneath the gauzy dress of green scattered with pink flowers across her breasts and hugging her waist. The same dress she wore yesterday when she materialized from the tree. I focused on her eyes and kept her gaze on me. We breathed deep together. After a few minutes, her eyes drained of the fear and filled with a sparkle in the indigo rim around the blue of her iris.

"Thank you," she whispered.

"Any time, sweet thing." I winked.

Briana puffed out a laugh and shook her head.

"So, um." I pointed my finger at her dress. "Did you bring other clothes with you?"

She glanced down. "No."

"My ma owns a small clothing store in town. Do you want to go get more clothes to wear while you're here?"

"I, ah. What about Arrow and Saoirse?" She flicked her hand at the forest.

"They'll be absent for hours. They screw like rabbits," I said. "Want to take a ride into town in my truck?"

Briana wrinkled her nose. "One would think Saoirse is in heat, but she can't be while pregnant."

"Fae have a heat?"

"Aye. I no longer do so donna get any ideas in your head."

Briana walked over to my Ford F-250.

More lies. A wolf shifter boasted a lot of perks. Didn't she realize we could scent lies? I should tell her, but then ... the dilemma. I opened my truck door for her. "What ideas would that be, princess?"

She climbed up the step onto the truck seat and pursed her lips.

I closed the door with a chuckle, strutted around the truck, and climbed into the driver's seat. With a turn of the key, my truck rumbled to life. I drove along the dirt driveway to the uncomfortable silence from Briana. Whatever freak out happened back there, it'd affected her badly.

"Do you like music?" I switched on the radio.

"I do. My mother is a sensational singer," Briana said. "Not to this type of music, though."

"Yeah? Do you sing too?"

"Aye. Not in the presence of an audience like her."

I hummed to the song on the radio. Briana hummed the tune, too. Her soft tunes soon stopped mine so I could hear her sweetness. I turned onto the main road of Crystal Creek, leaving the dirt road for the tarmac. The locals sat outside the café sipping on coffees and chatting, others wandered the small line of shops, ducking in and out of stores. I parked my truck near Kelly's Clothes and hopped out. I rounded the pickup and opened the door for Briana. She swept from the seat like the princess she was.

"Your mother owns this place?"

"Yeah." I opened the glass door of the store for her. I'd open a lot of doors for her if she'd just walk through the one to me as easily as she did the others. Who knew finding your mate would be so difficult? And exhilarating.

Briana stepped inside. I followed. I'd follow her to the ends of the Earth, let alone a woman's clothing store.

"Sheldon," Ma said, and rushed from behind the counter. "What are you doing in here?"

"Sledge, Ma." I bent down and kissed her cheek.

She patted my shoulder. "You'll always be my little Sheldon."

Briana's lips twitched, and she placed a hand over her mouth. Stupid name, Sheldon. It always reminded people of that character from the geeky show, and I was nothing like him.

"Ma, this is Saoirse's sister, Briana." I waved a hand between them. "Briana, this is my ma, Kelly Braidwood."

"Oh," Ma said. "Another Fae in town. Does Ray know?"

"Not yet. Briana arrived yesterday."

"Best you tell him before someone else does." Ma faced Briana. "You're as pretty as your sister."

"Thank you." Briana dipped her head. "I can see where Sheldon gets his good looks from."

Ma twittered and preened her dark hair at the compliment, but satisfaction filled my chest. Briana thought I was good looking.

"Briana's in town for a bit and needs some clothes. Can you help her?"

"Of course." Ma ran her gaze over Briana. "With a figure like yours, you'll be easy to fit for clothes. How long are you here for?"

"I intend to stay and help Saoirse with the birth."

"Are you a midwife?" Ma led Briana to a rack of pants.

"No. I have experience with Fae births, though." Briana wrinkled her nose at the pants. "I donna wear trousers."

"Dresses in winter? It's freezing here this time of year."

"Sheldon doesn't clothe himself for the weather." Briana nodded her head my way.

"That boy of mine will always do the opposite of what he's told."

"Come on, Ma." I groaned. "I'm not that bad."

Ma led Briana to a small rack with summer dresses. "This is all I have in stock of dresses. The summer clothes are only just beginning to filter into the store."

Briana slid a coat hanger from the rack and held up a dress of twilight blue. "'Tis short, these dresses."

"It's the fashion this year. Would you like to try them on?"

"No, they'll suffice." Briana selected three dresses and hung them over her arm.

"Here, let me take them for you." Ma grabbed the dresses and walked over to the counter. She rang up the clothes on the cash register.

I handed over my credit card.

Ma's eyebrows rose, but she said nothing to me. She turned to Briana instead and ran her gaze over her in a new light. "Lovely to meet you, Briana. I'm sure we'll see more of you around town?"

"Aye," Brianna said, taking the bag Ma held out to her. "'Twas a pleasure to meet you."

I opened the glass door and Briana swept outside into the misting rain of a winter's day. I dashed for the car while Briana strode over without a care for the falling rain. She tilted her face to the sky and licked her lips. My cock twitched. I averted my gaze from my mate before I embarrassed myself by walking through town with a raging hard-on in a pair of work out pants.

"Let's go," I growled, opening the car door for her.

Briana dropped her startled gaze to me. I avoided looking at her. She climbed into the truck, and I slammed the door. At least she hadn't tried on the short dresses. *Who knows how I would have reacted to watching her do that?*

My wolf was ready to sink his teeth into her neck and claim her. I rocked my head to clear the haze shifting before my eyes and not from the misting rain. With more force than necessary, I wrenched open the driver's door and climbed inside. I shoved the truck into reverse and tore off through town.

Briana pursed her lips.

It only made me want her more.

Her natural floral scent filled the truck. Anger marked the fragrant aroma of her silent desire for me. My cock swelled. Angry sex with my mate would be so hot. Any sex would be. A growl rumbled from my throat. My wolf wanted out and out now.

I skidded to a stop in the mud along Arrow's driveway.

"Go inside," I rumbled, clenching the steering wheel, and breathing hard through my mouth, but her aroma coated my tongue. I longed to taste her. All of her. From the tips of her dainty ears to her toes peeking out from under her dress and everything in between. Especially everything in between.

I ripped my t-shirt over my head and opened the door. Briana's gaze dropped to my bare chest. Her scent ripened further. Lush. I licked my lips.

She fumbled for the door handle. "Where are you going?"

I winked and reached for my pants.

Briana's breath quickened. Her chest heaved. My wolf growled at me to mark her as mine. I fought the savage beast inside me. Our mate needed more than a mating mark and hard sex. I needed to get away from Briana's scent to reason with him.

"A run. Are you staying for the strip show?" I eased the top of my pants down a fraction.

Her eyes widened.

I spun around and inched my pants over my ass. The car door slammed behind me, and the front door of the house opened and slammed too. I let out a relieved breath. For the wolf might have won if she'd stayed to watch me strip. I ripped off my pants and shifted in a swift change of contorting limbs and fur. My wolf let out a howl of freedom and frustration. I raced into the forest. Away from Briana's enticing scent.

Away from my mate.

The forest flickered by in a rush of browns and greens. Leaf litter crunched under my paws. I hurdled a fallen tree and burst through the foliage onto the sandy shore of the lake. The water rippled with the raindrops, falling harder with a pitter-patter of water on water. I ran the perimeter of the lake away from Crystal Creek into the wilderness of the Australian forest. With each step away from my mate's alluring scent, my wolf settled from the roaring need to mark her.

I slowed to a walk.

'All right, buddy. You got to stop fighting me. We'll claim our mate. She needs time first.'

My wolf growled.

'I know, I know. I'm aching for her too.'

He whimpered in agreement.

I prowled the shore of the lake now the rain had stopped. This far from town, the wilderness was even wilder.

'You trying to bite her won't win her over.'

My lip curled in a snarl.

'She needs to come to us. You've met her. You know I'm right.'

I paused and studied a paw print in the sandy soil. Not a wolf. I sniffed the print. Fresh with the tang of a cat and more. A familiarity that made me cock my head. I swung my gaze to the tree line. High in the trees, a dark shadow lay on the branches. Green eyes stared back at me. The enormous cat blinked. Flicked its tail. There was no way I'd take on a big cat. *What the hell was a black jaguar doing in Australia? And with a scent so familiar?* The cat rose and slunk along the tree branch. With a tremendous leap, it jumped into the next tree, ran down the trunk, and faded into the forest.

I let out a small whine. My wolf wanted to chase the running cat, but I knew better than to mess with a jaguar. And finally, my wolf sensed I was right about our mate, too. He settled with a calmness I'd never experienced from the beast. I hoped, once we possessed our mate in entirety, he'd settle into this calm forever because fighting him all the time was wearing me down.

CHAPTER SIX

BRIANA

I SLAMMED THE FRONT door, muttering under my breath.

Saoirse poked her head out of the kitchen. "Where have you been?" She eyed me. "What's wrong?"

"Wolf shifters are maniacal. One minute they're helping you buy clothes, the next they're running off into the forest." I flapped my hand at the front door sending the shopping bag flying every which way.

"Sledge took you shopping?" Her eyebrows rose.

Arrow slid behind Saoirse and peered over her shoulder, his golden eyes alight in the way I was becoming accustomed.

"Aye." I tossed the bag on the floor and joined them in the kitchen.

Arrow returned to cooking and Saoirse perched on a barstool. I slid onto the stool beside her.

"What did you get?" she asked.

"Dresses. More half a dress than a proper dress. Where do you get yours from? They're like the ones you wore in the Summer Court."

"Arrow sews mine." She swept her hair back from her shoulders.

"Your mate cooks and sews?" I studied Arrow anew. Perhaps wolf shifters weren't all bad if you could put up with their mood swings.

Arrow spun around from the stovetop and wielded the wooden spoon in his hand. "Honey, I told you not to tell anyone."

"Whoops." She covered her mouth with her hand. "Sorry."

I laughed. "I won't say a word if you make me dresses too."

"Blackmail?" Arrow arched an eyebrow.

"We are family, after all." I grinned.

Arrow eyed my dress. "I can't do little flowers like those, but I can sew the same style."

"Perfect." I clapped my hands. "How long until you can make them?"

"A week or two." He shrugged.

"Dia, I'll be stuck wearing half a dress for a week."

"You could have purchased a tracksuit," he said.

"Pants?" I spluttered.

Saoirse nudged me with her elbow. "He doesn't get our penchant for dresses, but he appreciates them."

I rolled my eyes.

Arrow chuckled and turned back to the stovetop. "So, you and Sledge?"

"There is no me and Sledge." I sat up straight.

"Right..." Arrow said.

I huffed. "Do you wolf shifters always run off as a wolf?"

Arrow scrubbed the back of his neck. "There are times we do." He moved the saucepan from the stovetop and ladled the contents onto three plates. "We're part beast and the animal rides us hard when it's hidden inside, in particular at times of stress."

"Stress? What is Sledge stressed about?"

Arrow placed two plates on the table for me and Saoirse. His golden gaze caught and held mine. "Women are stressful."

"We are not." Saoirse seethed through her clenched teeth.

Arrow covered her hands with his. "Honey, you get us all tangled up in knots even when you don't mean to."

Saoirse leaned forward and kissed him.

I cleared my throat before they forgot I was in the room. "What did you cook for dinner?"

"Pumpkin risotto with leek and spinach," Arrow said with a flourish. "And for me, a big thick juicy pork steak thanks to Sledge. Wild pig has the best flavor." He smacked his lips.

"You don't mind his meat-eating?" I asked Saoirse.

"No." She dug her fork into the risotto. "He brushes his teeth after eating meat before kissing me."

Arrow flashed her a toothy smile. One that said he'd be brushing his teeth straight away to kiss her. I was in for another long night of listening to their lovemaking.

Sledge's truck rumbled to life in the driveway. A part of me wanted to run outside and make sure he was all right and hadn't taken on another feral boar. The other part wanted to rub against his nakedness. But the part that won out, was the one that hardened herself against ever having a mate again.

I thumped the pillow for the umpteenth time and climbed out of bed. In the darkness of the night, I rummaged in the shopping bag and slid on one of the new dresses then stomped out the front door. Saoirse's screams of pleasure filled the house. This was ridiculous. *How talented were wolf shifters at sex to make her scream like that?*

I'd never had a lover make me scream aloud. Even my former mate never induced that much passion in our lovemaking. We'd been good together though. Those memories had lasted me hundreds of years. They'd last me hundreds more. I'd never forgotten him.

My breath gusted out in an icy blast in the night air. I walked without thought through the dark forest. The occasional glimpse of small orange eyes peered back at me through the treetops. Leaves rustled in the animal's haste to hide. I wouldn't harm the animals, but fear of the unknown kept them alive. My fear left a mark. I rubbed my wrist, remembering what caused that fear.

A couple of miles walking through the forest, and it ended at the edge of town. The streetlights shone a golden hue along the quaint streets. I walked closer as the scent of cooking drifted from the main square in the center of the town. I slowed and inched closer. The locals were converged under and around a white gazebo talking and eating. What appeared to be the remains of a pig hung from a stainless-steel spit over hot coals. On the edge of the square someone had placed a half barrel for a fire brought in for the occasion whatever that was. A group of men huddled around the remaining coals glowing bright red in the darkness of the night.

I took an involuntary step back.

"Hi," a girl's voice squeaked.

I flinched and snapped my gaze to the girl on the right of me. *How did she sneak up on me?*

"Are you the new Fae in town?"

I slanted my head. *How did she recognize me?* "I am."

She sneered, her pointed teeth flashing under the streetlights. "I'm Heidi."

"Nice to meet you, Heidi. Should you be talking to strangers by yourself?"

She scowled in the only way a child could.

"You're not a stranger. Your name is Briana."

"Is that right?" I curled my arms over my chest. *Who had she been talking to?* "How old are you?"

"I'm twelve, but I'll be thirteen next month." She stood taller.

My heart spasmed. Thirteen. The same age as my daughter was. No ... I couldn't remember. I put a hand to my head to hold the memories back.

"I'm having a party. Will you come?" Heidi asked.

"Me?" I swept my hand to my chest.

"Yeah. I want a gigantic party so I'm asking everyone."

Laugher bubbled from my mouth. "I suppose you're only thirteen once."

"It's a big occasion for wolf shifters." She twirled her long dark hair. "It's the age we're finally able to join the hunting packs."

"You hunt?"

"Well, we are wolves." She flashed her pointed teeth. "What's your power?"

"I can manipulate plants."

She frowned. "Is that all? I thought it'd be something big. Fae aren't as good as wolf shifters."

"Big?" I rose my eyebrows. "Like this?"

I flourished my hands calling my power to draw on one of the tall claret ash trees lining the streets. The tree creaked and glowed a luminous green. Then the tree shuffled closer to us. I flicked my hands, and the branches extended around Heidi in a tree hug. The girl disappeared inside the gnarled wood of the branches and the dark, lacy leaves. I twisted my hand, and the leaves parted for me to see her face.

She scowled. Behind us, masculine chuckles drifted through the air.

"Big enough for you?" I laughed.

"Let me go." She squirmed in the branches. "I hate you."

Her words hurt. I twirled my hand, and the tree returned to where it'd been. Heidi brushed her thick red jacket and dusted a few leaves from her shoulders and hair.

"Don't make fun of a Fae's power." I called my power back until my hands no longer glowed.

Heidi huffed out a lungful of air and breathed a small cloud of mist in the night air and plonked herself on the curb. I sat beside her tugging the short dress as far as I could. Pants would have been good right about now with the breeze wafting up my dress.

"Don't tell Sledge or the Alpha I was a brat."

"I won't." I touched her hand.

She peered up at me through her thick fringe as though she couldn't make up her mind to hate me or be intrigued by me. A loud thud echoed across the town. We swung our gazes to the town center. The fire popped and sparked to life around a log. The orange and red flames crackled. Sparks flew in the smoke wafting up into the air. I rubbed my wrist. The flames grew bigger. Coldness coated every inch of my skin when Fae didn't feel the cold. I scrambled to my feet and ran into the forest away from the fire.

"Wait," Heidi yelled.

I didn't wait. I ran. The winter wind slapped my cheeks and seeped into my fear-riddled body. My feet turned to lead. Each step grew heavier and heavier. Colder and colder. The pounding in my ears from my heart made my vision blur. My face smacked into a wall of solid muscle.

"Easy," Sledge said.

I wobbled and sunk to the forest floor. Sledge kneeled facing me.

"Bree, sweetheart, breathe," he coaxed.

I rubbed my wrists.

Sledge held his hands out palms up. "Give me your pain."

I shook my head. The pain and the fear were mine. No one could take it away.

"You don't need to be strong all the time."

"I do," I whispered. "I'm the oldest sister. They all look up to me."

He wriggled his fingers. "Put your wrists here. Nothing else. I won't do anything to touch you other than you placing your wrists in my hands. It's all your choice."

I peered into his earnest face alight with truth in the moonlit forest and placed my wrists in his hands. Warmth like nothing I'd ever experienced poured from his touch. The ache in my flesh eased, then disappeared for the first time in centuries.

"How?" I gasped.

He held his hands still and smiled at my wrists in his palms. "You understand how."

I glanced away. I couldn't admit what we were. That he was my fated mate. And I was his.

"What happened? Why the freak out?"

"The fire..."

"Ah." He sat on the ground opposite me with my wrists still in his palms.

"What has Saoirse told you about me?" I sat up straighter but didn't take my hands away from him. I liked the soothing calmness of his touch too much.

"Nothing and I wouldn't ask her." He frowned. "When she marked Arrow, he muttered something about a fire and your people burning before he passed out."

"Oh." I wet my lips.

"I've seen enough animals burn in fires to understand it's a horrendous sight."

"Aye." A tear slipped from my right eye.

"It haunts you. The smell. The screams. The powerless feeling."

Another tear slipped free onto my cheek.

"How long have you been haunted, Bree?"

"Too long." I lifted my chin.

"I want to wrap you in my arms, and comfort you from your nightmares," he said. "But I won't until you ask me to."

I breathed deep, drawing in his spicy scent. It calmed and excited me at the same time. I wanted to experience what being comforted in his arms was like. It'd been so long since a man had held me for anything other than sex. But what if I lost him?

"Did your wolf enjoy his run earlier?" I asked instead of giving into my desires.

Sledge laughed at my unimaginative change of topic. "He did, and he didn't. But he's willing to admit I'm right now."

I slid my hands from Sledge's warmth and stood brushing the dirt and leaves from my dress.

"Do I want to comprehend what you're right about?"

Sledge ran his heated gaze along my bare legs. Lust slammed into my stomach in an instant. He slicked his lips with the tip of his tongue. My body quivered with the need for his mouth. He inhaled and rose with his nose inches from my legs, up to my body, and to within kissing distance of my lips.

"Your scent..." he muttered.

My nipples tightened into hard peaks beneath the scratchy cotton fabric of the dress.

He blinked and stepped back. "Perhaps not. Otherwise, you'll fight me as much as my wolf did."

His words sent images of us fighting with the staffs into my mind and then us landing in a pile of sweaty limbs ripping off clothes and fighting for who would be on top for sex. My body slicked with need and moisture.

"I'll walk you back to Arrow's house."

"I can find my way," I said, and I strode off into the forest.

Sledge whistled.

I paused and faced him.

He nodded his head in the opposite direction I'd been heading. "This way."

I folded my arms over my chest to cover my hard nipples and stomped over to him.

"Sweetheart, you're all kinds of sexy when you're angry."

I rolled my eyes.

"Practice your pickup lines on other women, Sledge. They won't work on me." I moved through the forest with Sledge at my side.

"Did Saoirse tell you about the pickup line I used on her?"

"You attempted to pick up my sister?" My stomach churned with anger and jealousy.

Sledge laughed. "Damn it, woman, I'm hard as a rock now with how pissed you are, and it's making it difficult to walk."

"I can't believe your gall." I shoved through the branches and stumbled into the driveway of Arrow's house.

His laugh followed me to the front door.

He slapped a hand to the door, leaned close to my ear, and whispered, "Sweet dreams, sweet thing."

A shiver danced down my spine from his breath on my skin and the desire I'd experienced for him roared to life. Sledge shifted his hand and opened the door for me. I slipped inside, thankful it was quiet, and made my way to my bedroom.

This wouldn't do. I couldn't stay here and go wandering every night only to end up spending time with Sledge. I'd have to find somewhere else to stay. Surely there was accommodation to be acquired in town?

CHAPTER SEVEN
BRIANA

I SAT ON THE shore of the lake and watched Saoirse play in the cold water. Arrow sat beside me as reluctant as me to go in the icy water. His expression exuded patient love though. He'd go in the water if Saoirse asked him. She didn't though. She was content playing by herself with her power.

"Did Sledge try to pick up Saoirse?" I blurted out the one thought which had been in my mind since Sledge said it last night.

Arrow chuckled. "Not in an actual sense."

"What do you mean?"

"Sledge and I used these pickup routines where one of us would be extra arrogant to the woman and the other would swoop in and save her."

I coughed. "Women fell for that?"

Arrow shrugged. "Humans, yes. Saoirse, no. She saw through our act right from the start."

"So, her and Sledge..." I fluttered my hand at Saoirse.

"Fuck, no. I understood she was my mate from the moment I scented her." Arrow picked up a rock and tossed it into the water. "I likely would have hurt Sledge if he'd tried anything with Saoirse."

I picked up a stick and drew in the sandy soil.

"Why do you ask?" he asked.

"No reason."

"You Fae women are so reluctant to the idea of a mate it's no wonder your race is declining."

I dropped the stick. "What did you say?"

"I said—"

He paused as I stood in a flourish.

"I heard you."

"Then why ask me to repeat it?"

"Because I think you're onto something."

"I am?" He stood.

"Yes, other than my sister." I smirked.

Arrow shrugged. "I'm not apologizing for making her happy."

"I wouldn't want you to. She looks the happiest I've ever seen her. So, thank you for making my sister happy, but I can't stay here another night and listen to you two."

Arrow laughed.

Saoirse swooshed out of the water in her pink bathing suit, her prominent stomach on display. "What's funny?"

Arrow hauled her into his arms. "Seems we're keeping your sister up at night."

Saoirse had the good grace to look apologetic. "Sorry, Briana."

"Is there accommodation in town? I can stay there at night and leave you two to you know."

"Aye." Saoirse flicked a glance at Arrow.

"There's one place. It's a family owned bed and breakfast. Has a long history of being the best and only place to stay for out of town shifters. I suppose an out of town Fae is the same thing," he said. "We'll drive you there when Saoirse gets dressed."

"How do you swim in this weather?"

Saoirse shrugged. "Fae don't feel the cold."

"Still..." I flicked a glance at the lake. The water was inky black.

"It rejuvenates me, and the baby likes it, but he prefers the waterfall. Will you come with me to see it soon?"

"Aye. There's no hurry. I'll be here for as long as you need me."

Saoirse sighed. "I need my family forever."

I wrapped an arm around her shoulders.

"Do you think Lorcan will come soon? I miss him so," she asked.

"He misses you too," I assured her.

We walked back through the forest to their house. Saoirse and Arrow disappeared to their bedroom. I collected my small shopping bag with the two other dresses and gathered up my Fae dress. Perhaps I could wash it at the accommodations, then I could wear it while waiting for Arrow to sew me new dresses. I almost laughed aloud at the thought of telling Father Saoirse's mate sewed.

My spine stiffened. No surprise Father hadn't come looking for me. I couldn't provide him with heirs, much to his chagrin. It hurt he didn't care enough about his eldest daughter to search for me. I shouldn't fault him too much. He'd found me tied to a stake, and together with Lorcan and Saoirse, they'd saved me from burning to death along with Mother and Aislinn, but they'd been too late to save my grandparents. I wish they could have saved my mate, Donagh. His warrior ways led to his and our daughter's demise in the worst possible way.

I rubbed my wrist, then paused remembering the warmth from Sledge's hands on my old wounds. The peace and calm that surrounded me from his touch. Then the burning lust coursing through my body. Sledge was my fated mate, but losing a chosen mate was so painful. If I lost another mate, my heart would bleed in a river of crimson tears and my mind might shatter from the agony.

"You ready, Briana?" Saoirse called through the bedroom door.

"Aye." I flung wide the door and strode outside.

Arrow helped Saoirse into his vehicle and buckled her seatbelt.

I climbed into the back seat. "How is the wee tot today?"

Saoirse caressed her stomach. "He's good and kicking up a storm like usual."

Arrow climbed into the driver's seat and started the truck. The drive down the dirt track was bumpy. I bounced around on the back seat wishing I'd walked to town. The short dress rode up my thighs. Humans were ridiculous with their attire. I suppose underwear helped in these situations. Those things bugged Fae, so we didn't wear them.

"Here we are." Arrow slammed the car into the park. "I texted Sledge. He's expecting you and has a room ready."

"Why would you text Sledge?"

"He owns the place." Arrow nodded at the house. "His grandmother gave him the place to run when his grandfather retired as Alpha and Sledge's dad took over as pack Alpha. She told him it would keep him out of trouble."

Arrow laughed and Saoirse giggled.

"And this is the only place to stay?"

"Aye." Saoirse placed a hand over her mouth.

I narrowed my eyes. Scheming sister. I straightened my shoulders. It was either go back to their house and listen to them have sex all night, or spend the night in the same house as Sledge. At least here I could hide in my room.

"Thank you." I opened the back door.

"We'll pick you up in the morning," Saoirse called out.

"I'll walk." I shuddered at the idea of riding in Arrow's vehicle again. At least Sledge's truck hadn't bounced like his.

I crossed the road to the two-story white house surrounded by a lethal-looking picket fence. I'd like to give those pickets a whirl like the staffs. As I opened the front gate, the hinges creaked as though it was old. I walked up to the front door. Before I could knock, the door swung open. Sledge grinned, dressed in nothing but a towel. Water dripped off his muscular shoulders onto the roundness of his pecks.

I swallowed the knot in my throat. Heat raced through my body. Perhaps a dip in the lake would've been a good idea.

"Sorry, I thought I'd have time for a shower before you arrived," he said.

I opened my mouth. Shut it. Opened it again. "Arrow drives like a maniac."

"He does." Sledge stood aside. "Welcome to Wolf's Lodge Hotel."

"Subtle." I stepped inside the house.

"Everything about me is subtle."

My gaze dropped to the towel around his waist. There was nothing subtle about Sledge. Least of all what he had hidden beneath the towel.

"Sweetheart, if you keep looking at the towel like you want to rip it off then you'll force me to leave it on all night just to see the sparkle in your eyes."

"I, ah." I raised my gaze to his face. Dia, it was getting harder to resist him.

"Speechless too?" He dropped his hand to the towel. "I might always wear a towel."

I rolled my eyes. "Where's my room?"

Sledge chuckled. "Damn, woman, way to ruin a man's ego." He strutted through the house and opened a door. "Here you go, Princess."

I slipped into the room, careful to not brush against the towel and make it fall from his waist. The room was spectacular. A bed sat at the end of the room elevated on a platform with steps leading to the thick mattress. A pair of animal hide chairs sat at the bottom of the platform and faced the large glass door overlooking the lush green gardens.

"Dinner is in an hour."

"I assume you will replace the towel for dinner?" I lifted an eyebrow.

Sledge waggled his eyebrows and strutted away.

I closed the door and opened the glass door into the garden. The plants called to me. I stepped outside and inhaled a calming breath of nature. One then two breaths eased me. I could do this. I could stay in the house of a man who fate had chosen for me and pretend he wasn't. *What choice did I have?*

I skidded to a stop in the timber kitchen and combined dining room. Two women sat at the long oak table. I crossed the room to their stares.

"Briana, this is Eloise and Clara from England. They joined our pack not that long ago."

"Hello." I drew out a chair and sat at the table.

Sledge appeared laid back and at ease with the women in his kitchen, but the air in the room was not one of comfort. Was it my fault? Or was it these women?

Sledge sat at the table and pointed at the food. "Help yourself."

I picked up a small bread roll and picked off pieces. Sledge piled his plate with food, while the women placed a generous helping on theirs. The two women eyed me across the table.

"Don't worry, I didn't make the food," Sledge said. "Clara here did. She's my new cook, and Eloise always tags along with her friend."

"You aren't staying here in the hotel too?"

"No." Eloise chomped on a piece of roll. "We did when we first arrived, but we moved into our own place."

I relaxed a little. "Do you have any other guests?"

"No, just you." Sledge winked.

"You didn't need to hire a cook for me. I can make my food."

"It's part of the hotel package."

Clara giggled. "We had to make our food when we stayed here."

"Shut up." Sledge threw a bread roll at her face. "This is a five-star hotel."

Clara dodged it with ease.

"Five stars from who?" Clara giggled again.

The woman annoyed me with her giggling. The other woman sat in stony silence with hostility radiating from her pores. I didn't bother making conversations with these two while I ate, and the less I spoke to Sledge the better.

Eloise scraped her plate clean and shoved back her chair. "I'll see you later. I'm meeting up with someone."

"Yeah?" Sledge asked. "Who?"

I tilted my head. Why did he want to know who she was meeting? Did he like her? Or was there more going on here that I didn't know about?

"None of your business." She stomped to the back door and escaped into the night.

Sledge sat back in his seat with a frown. "Who is she meeting, Clara?"

"I don't know." Clara chewed her lip. "She's been strange since we arrived here."

"In what way?" he asked.

"She used to tell me everything, now she skulks around and hides things from me. I thought us coming here to find mates would be good. We've been friends for life, and I figured our kids would grow up together. But..." She worried her bottom lip between her teeth.

Sledge reached across the table and placed his hand on Clara's arm. My power surged to my hands. Sledge's lips twitched. I shoved my hands under the table. Clara seemed oblivious to my raging jealousy.

"You've met your mate," Sledge stated.

"I have." Clara perked up. "Jonathon."

"Our newest recruit? Well, congrats."

"Thanks. He wants me to live with him, but I'm worried about Eloise being by herself."

"I'll keep an eye on Eloise. You go be with your mate as fate intends."

Sledge met my gaze across the table. The man was sneaky. Underhanded. And quite right. A mate should be with their mate. Except I couldn't go through the pain again.

I shoved back my chair and stood. "I'm going to bed."

My stomach rumbled. I rose from the platform bed, slid on a thick white plush robe I found folded on top of the chest of drawers, and left the bedroom. I should have eaten more than a bread roll at dinner, but the jealousy coating my throat made swallowing hard when Sledge put his hand on Clara's arm. He'd awoken feelings in me I hadn't experienced for centuries, and I wanted to keep my feelings asleep. Keep my needs and wants hidden as I'd managed for the longest of times. Otherwise...

A soft murmur sounded from the kitchen.

Shite, is he awake?

To stay or head back to my room?

"I know you're out there, Bree," Sledge said.

Double shite.

I padded into the kitchen on my bare feet. At least this robe fell to my ankles, not like the dress I'd worn earlier. I wouldn't back down. I hadn't made it this long without my strong will. The kitchen was dark except for the pale light of the full moon through the window. Sledge faced the window bathed, in the ethereal glow of the moon, leaving me with an uninhibited view of his firm back and the twin globes of his tight buttocks in glowing white boxer shorts.

My ridiculous heart quickened.

He turned and afforded me with a view of his glorious front. I kept my gaze on the bundle in his arms and walked into the room for a closer look at what he held. A small gray fluffy koala cub nestled to his muscular chest.

"He's so adorable." I touched a hand to my heart. A twinge of jealousy ran through me the koala enjoyed his embrace when I kept denying I wanted it for myself. I cleared my throat. "Is he all right?"

"He will be now. He was a little woozy when he came into the rehab center." Sledge transferred the sleeping cub into a crate next to the table. "It's why I wanted to check on him."

Why did he have to be so kind and caring?

Every moment I spent with him, he awoke more feelings. I walked over to the refrigerator. Better for me to stay away from him as much as possible while we were in the same house together. He followed me and placed a hand on the refrigerator.

"What are you doing?"

"I'm hungry." I turned.

"You should have eaten dinner." He tapped the refrigerator door.

His spicy scent surrounded me and filled the places I comprehended fate meant him to satisfy. If I let him. My body desired everything about him. I couldn't stop the rush of need boiling in my body from his nearness.

"I wasn't hungry then."

"You missed out on blueberry pie for dessert too. There's plenty left if you'd like some now."

"Blueberry?" I perked up. Blueberry was a Fae favorite. "Would you like a piece too?"

He chuckled, lowered his nose to the side of my neck, and breathed in deep. "I want a piece."

Heat coiled low in my body until an ache radiated with insistence I give in to our fate. To our cravings, to lose ourselves in the other's body as mates.

He inhaled again and smirked. "Are you ready to give me a piece?"

This close, I couldn't deny my attraction to him, my skin rippled in awareness under the robe so hypersensitive that it felt chafed against the soft material. The night air drifted up from the tiled floor and slithered up my calves, to my thighs, and higher to the damp moisture building within. Heat and desire coursed through my body in his presence. I wet my lips.

His gaze darkened. Intense and thrilling. The wolf flitted in the depths of his eyes, but he didn't lose control like yesterday. Instead, the wildness of the wolf excited me more.

My body swayed closer, drawn to the intensity of Sledge. Of what he'd mean to me if I let him in. Fear lanced my heart with a blinding clarity—I couldn't give in to the lure of Sledge.

"No." I pushed at his naked chest. Dia, I shouldn't have touched him. Heat burned my palms with rightness and my power caused them to glow, wanting to mark him as mine. Claim him as my mate. I gasped. "Give me space, you overgrown puppy."

Sledge stepped back and held up his hands.

I struggled to call my power back. It tugged and enticed me to step closer to Sledge, to pin him down and sear him with my mark.

"Overgrown puppy indeed." He peered down.

I followed the direction of his gaze. His tight white boxer shorts strained with the enormous size of his overgrown... I snapped my gaze up to his face.

"Don't worry, Bree. This overgrown puppy won't share his bone with you until you ask." He winked and sauntered out of the kitchen.

I sagged against the refrigerator. Need coated my insides to have him share himself with me. I forced my legs together and opened the refrigerator. The icy air hit my warm face. *Why did the self-assured, wolf shifter appeal to me so?* Dia, help me fend him off for the next few months instead of begging for his 'bone'.

CHAPTER EIGHT

SLEDGE

I YAWNED AND SCRAPED a hand over my rough jaw as I leaned against the kitchen counter. Sleep was impossible after encountering Briana in the kitchen last night. I thought for a moment she was about to kiss me, about to give in to the call of mates. But then she'd shoved me away, shattering my brief flare of hope. My wolf whimpered.

'I know.'

He quietened, and I sipped my coffee. At least he made things easier for me now. My mate's sweet scent drifted into the kitchen, but I didn't turn around from the window overlooking the garden around my hotel. Maybe a day of hard gardening would ease my raging needs. I could chop the fallen tree, stack the wood for next year's winter. I wouldn't burn any wood in the fireplace with Briana in the hotel. There was no way I'd cause her another freak out. How she'd gone so long without facing her fears was a wonder.

Briana kneeled at the crate housing the small koala who'd lost his mother in the recent wildfires. "He's cute even with those lethal-looking claws."

I risked turning to face her. My fingers tightened around the mug. She wore another of the short dresses leaving her long legs on display. My wolf wanted to lick them. I agreed with him. I adjusted the growing bulge in my jeans.

Briana peeked up at me through her lashes.

Such a submissive position. My wolf chuffed in happiness. Briana's eyes widened.

"How does a wolf shifter care for koalas? I thought you'd want to eat them."

I chuckled. "Koalas don't taste the best."

She scrambled to her feet, affording me a view of her curvaceous thighs.

"Joking." I loved teasing her. "I don't know what koalas taste like. We stick to the feral pigs when we hunt. Other than that, we get our meat at the butcher like people."

"Humans." She hissed.

"Easy there, the town is wolf shifter territory."

"No humans?"

"No. We get the occasional tourist, but we encourage them to keep moving. Which also means I don't have many guests now wolf numbers are so low."

"Your Alpha runs a tight pack. I should meet him. My presence in his town wouldn't have gone unnoticed."

My stomach dropped. Introducing her to Dad would go one of two ways. I didn't like those odds.

My fingers tightened on the mug as I sculled my coffee. "I suppose I could take you to meet him after breakfast."

She rose her eyebrows. My hesitation must be clear in my voice.

"What would you like to eat? I have cereal, toast, coffee."

Briana wrinkled her nose. "Another piece of blueberry pie?"

"Pie for breakfast?" I opened the refrigerator and muttered. "I wouldn't mind eating your pie for breakfast."

A chair scraped across the tiles. I drew the pie out and shut the refrigerator. Briana sat at the table, a slight pink tinged her cheeks. I slid the pie onto the table with a plate and cutlery and left her to it. Walking back to the counter, I shoved bread in the toaster and made another cup of coffee. I'd need the caffeine today. The toast popped. I slapped a slathering of peanut butter on top, then sat at the table opposite Briana. She slid a fork into her mouth. Even that was sexy. I shifted on the seat.

"You're drinking more coffee?" She eyed the mug.

"Yeah, I didn't get much sleep."

"Oh." She wiped her fingers on the tabletop. "I slept well after eating this delicious pie. Did Clara make it?" Her body stiffened.

I grinned. My mate was jealous. She had nothing to be jealous of but at least it showed she was interested in me. How would she feel is she knew Dad had intended me to choose Clara or Eloise as a mate?

"No. Arrow made the pie. He makes them for Saoirse."

"He's sweet to her." She licked blueberry from her lips.

"Wolf shifters are sweet to their mates. We may be half-wild beasts, but we treat our mates with the utmost care in whatever they need." I chomped the last of my toast and licked my fingers. "Even if it goes against our nature."

Briana's scent ripened as it did around me, but the times she lusted after me, it filled her scent with a mouth-watering aroma. I licked my lips. Damn, what I wouldn't give to taste her and pleasure her. I bet she'd be as wild as my wolf in bed. She was so restrained everywhere else, there was no way she'd hold back in the throes of passion. I'd make sure of it.

I stretched my legs under the table coming close to Briana's legs but not touching her since I'd stick to my promise and wait until she asked me to touch her. The longing was palpable. I might have balls as blue as the blueberries in her pie by then, but she was worth the wait.

She finished her pie and licked the fork clean. "What are you thinking?"

"I'm thinking," I said lowering my voice, "about how many times I can make you scream with pleasure when you finally ask me to touch you."

"I donna scream." She placed the fork on the dinner table with careful, controlled movements.

"No?" I raised an eyebrow. "It'll be so much fun when you do under my lips, my tongue, my teeth, my fingers, my—"

"Sledge." She moaned my name like I imagined her doing in bed.

Her scent grew stronger. Her chest heaved under the flimsy summer dress of pale green pushing her hard nipples into the fabric. My teeth ached to sink into her soft mounds. They'd be the first place I'd bite her after marking her neck.

I placed my hand on the table next to Briana's hand. So close, but not touching. Her little finger twitched. Inched closer. I held my breath. *Ask me and we'd end our torture.* I shoved my plate aside and leaned over the table, my other hand landed on the back of her chair.

Briana lifted her chin. Her lips parted. I breathed again, mingling with her warm breath. This close to our mate, my wolf brushed against my skin. Her little finger stroked against mine. Sparks zapped. She tilted her head. Her lashes fluttered closed. She waited for me to close the distance. I couldn't unless she asked me.

"Ask me," I murmured.

She kept her eyes close, and shook her head barely missing my lips with hers. I groaned and thrust back gripping the edge of the table. My nails exploded into claws and scraped against the timber surface. Briana opened her eyes and stared at my hands.

"I won't hurt you." I dug my claws in deeper. "It's not possible."

She placed her hands on her flushed cheeks. "I almost kissed you."

"Almost," I grunted.

She dropped her hands to her lap and dropped her chin too. "I'm sorry."

"Sweetheart, look at me."

Briana's pale blue eyes rimmed with indigo snapped to my face.

"You never need to be sorry for anything you do to me. I'm yours."

"Sledge." She swallowed, her gaze flickering around my face. "I..."

I released my hard grip on the table. "Don't deny it, Bree. You feel it. I feel it. Whatever is holding you back, we'll work through it."

"I don't know if I can." She rubbed her wrist.

I held my hands out palms up. "Give me your pain. You've held onto it long enough."

With a shaky breath, she settled her wrists in my upturned hands. A sigh left her lips. The tension left my body. Doing anything to help my mate soothed me and my wolf. If only she'd let me help her more, I'd soothe every trouble and every pain. I'd let nothing hurt her again.

"What happened with your wrists?"

She snapped her hands away and stood.

I sighed. Too much too soon. I gathered up our breakfast dishes and placed them in the dishwasher.

"I'll take you to see the Alpha, then I'll drop you at Arrow's house."

"Thank you, Sledge." She dipped her head.

I strode through the house to the front door and opened it for Briana. She walked past me, leaving a trail of her flowery scent in my wake. My wolf snapped at me, but I shut him down, having him riled for a meeting with Dad would only add to the likelihood of him being a jerk meeting another Fae.

Briana waited for me to open my truck door. She climbed up into the cab flashing the expanse of her legs. I shut the door before I reached out and touched what I couldn't yet. Yet. I kept telling myself. It was only a matter of time. Time immortals possessed no matter how urgent the need to claim my mate.

I checked the time, climbed into the driver's seat, and drove the short distance through the streets of Crystal Creek to the mayor's office, also known as the Alpha's headquarters to us wolf shifters. I parked opposite the red brick building and took a calming breath.

"Do you not get along with your Alpha?" Briana asked.

"It's complicated." I opened my door before she asked more questions.

She waited for me to open her door, so different to the women these days, and I led the way to the office. A bell chimed as I opened the office door.

The receptionist, Jessa, grinned and twirled her pen around her fingers. "Hi, Sledge."

"Hey, Jessa. Is the Alpha available?"

"He's always available for you." She flicked her gaze to Briana. "Let me tell him you and your guest are here." She scrambled from her desk and knocked on the office door before disappearing inside.

"She likes you." Briana frowned.

"Jessa?" I frowned too.

Briana nodded.

I scrubbed the back of my neck. I thought Jessa was over our time together as teenagers. Briana crossed her arms over her chest. The office door opened, and Jessa appeared.

"Head on in," Jessa said with another grin aimed my way.

I waved my hand for Briana to proceed and closed the door behind me. The stiff set of her shoulders told me I'd have to set things right with the Jessa thing. First, I had to introduce her to my dad.

The Alpha stood behind his desk and glared at me. "Took you long enough, son."

"Briana, this is Ray Braidwood, the pack Alpha."

Her eyes widened and flicked between me and my dad. She regained her composure and dipped a curtsy.

"My apologies for not attending to formalities sooner." Briana stepped forward and offered my father her hand.

He stared at her offering.

"It is custom to greet a princess with respect."

My dad bristled but took her hand and bowed his head over it. "Please take a seat."

Briana settled on the chair, her back straight, her expression observant. I sat beside her.

Dad settled in his chair. "As Alpha, I need to ask what you are doing in our town?"

Briana folded her hands over her knees. "I'm visiting my sister. I will stay for the birth of her child. She'll need a Fae to help her."

"We look after our pack members. Your sister is a pack member. We'll care for her during the birth." He placed his hands on the papers on his desk.

"Fae births are not like a human or wolf shifters. She'll need me."

"Very well." He shuffled the papers. "Do you intend to stay after the birth?"

"I have no intention of staying on Earth, but I'd visit from time to time."

My muscles hardened into steel. My mate stated no intention of staying. Not even though she understood I was her mate. My wolf snarled inside.

Dad's gaze flicked to me. "And you'll stay at my son's hotel during this time?"

"Aye. He's been very accommodating."

"I'm sure." Dad folded his arms over his massive chest.

We were similar in our appearance, from our dark hair to the thickness of our muscles. Even without the introduction she would have known we were related.

"Heidi told me she invited you to her birthday party," Dad said. "I expect you to attend."

"Aye. I'll obey your rules while in town."

"You met my sister?" I asked.

Briana swung her head my way. "I met a youngster the other night in the town square. I didn't realize she was your sister."

"Your power annoyed her," Dad said. "She wouldn't stop complaining about it and how you trapped her with a tree."

I rose an eyebrow. And here I thought I was special with Briana tying me up to a tree. My sister was upset with my mate. I loved my sister, but I'd wanted to introduce them after I'd claimed Briana. Now I wouldn't get the chance. I scraped my thighs with my fists. Working out my frustrations chopping wood with the axe looked mighty tempting right about now.

"Sledge," Dad snapped my name like he knew I wasn't paying attention. "You'll be of assistance to Briana while she's staying with us."

"Yeah," I grumbled. As if I needed him to tell me what to do. As his son he'd groomed me to follow in his steps as Alpha ever since I was born.

"Don't talk to your Alpha like that." Dad stood.

I stood too. The air bristled.

"Like what?" I clenched my fist.

Briana's soft touch on my hand jerked me out of my anger. She touched Dad's hand too.

"You might be pack Alpha, but family comes first. I've lived long enough to witness the demise of creatures' homes and loves because they forget this. Don't become a memory to those you love and who love you in return." She swallowed.

"Bree," I said opening my fist and willing her to place her palm in mine.

She wrenched her hands away from both of us. "I'd like to visit my sister now. I'll wait outside for you to finish your pack business." She strode from Dad's office, her head held high and her curvaceous legs taking her out of my sight.

"She's something else," Dad said, lowering himself into his desk chair with a creak of the well-used wheels.

"Yeah, she's exceptional."

Dad cleared his throat. "You like her?"

"What's not to like? She just put us in our place with a few words."

"She did at that." He chuckled. "It would impress your mom."

"Mom met her."

"She said."

I eyed my dad. A smirk stretched his lips.

"You recognize who she is?"

"Everyone in town knows she's your mate. Why did you take so long to introduce her to me?"

"She's complicated, and you're not always the loving father."

He forced back his chair. "For fuck's sake, Sledge. You don't understand the pressure of being an Alpha." He shoved a hand through his hair. "And you're always intent on doing the opposite of what I say."

He wasn't wrong, but the discomfort flashing through his eyes made me reevaluate my hostility toward him telling me what to do all the time.

"Dad?"

"Yeah?"

"You're not mad a Fae is my mate?"

"I would have preferred you pick one of the new wolf shifters." He sighed. "But we have no choice in who our fated mate is."

I nodded. "How do I win her over?"

Dad smirked. "Lots and lots of sex."

I puffed out a breath. "Shit, I promised her I wouldn't touch her until she asked."

Dad steepled his fingers. "Why would you do that? You appreciate how tactile wolves are."

"My wolf is not happy being so close to our mate and not touching her."

Dad slapped the desk. "There's your answer. Maybe you can get around your promise in wolf form?"

My wolf perked up. Yeah, he liked the idea, beast that he was. *Would she class rubbing against her in wolf form as touching?* It was worth a try. Briana could only shut me down like usual.

CHAPTER NINE
SLEDGE

"**J**ESSA AND I DATED in high school," I said in the quiet of my truck.

Briana's head swung my way from where she'd been staring out of the truck window in stony silence as we made our way to Arrow's house.

"She was the first girl I had sex with." I flicked her a glance to see how she took the news.

Her face softened into a smile.

Huh?

"We haven't ... I haven't ... I don't look at Jessa like that anymore."

Briana laughed lightly.

"You're a handsome man, Sledge. I'm certain you've had many women share your bed as I've had men in mine."

A growl rumbled out of my throat.

She patted my thigh. My cock twitched.

"So, you think I'm handsome." I winked.

She rolled her eyes. "Your ego has no boundaries."

"It's big like the rest of me." I shifted my jeans over my crotch.

Her cheeks tinged with pink.

"Why didn't you tell me the Alpha is your father?"

A change of subject meant I was getting to Briana. Maybe rubbing my wolf against her wasn't such a bad idea.

"It didn't cross my mind. Most wolf shifters know who I am." Growing up in a town the size of Crystal Creek meant everyone recognized who I was, and those in other towns also knew. The wolf shifter community in Australia wasn't large by any means.

"You didn't omit it on purpose?" she asked.

"I'll tell you anything you want to know."

"What's the story between you and your father?"

I groaned. "Going for the throat. You're harsh, sweetheart."

She rubbed her hands together. "Throats are one of the softest places to attack."

"Dad's an Alpha. He acts like a jerk sometimes, especially when bossing me around. It makes my wolf angry."

"Of course, your wolf is an alpha too. You're bound to come to blows."

She'd nailed the problem in one meeting.

"I don't help the matter. I tend to rile him up too."

"You sound like my brother Lorcan. He picks fights with Father."

"I'll get along well with your brother then." I grinned.

The truck rolled off the smooth bitumen for the bumpy dirt track to Arrow's house, but I'd fitted my truck with exceptional shock absorbers.

"No doubt you'll meet him one day. Lorcan and Saoirse are close."

"What about you? Who are you closest to?"

"I don't know if I'm close to any of my siblings. We get along for the most part, but the Summer Court is tense now."

"Why's that?"

She swallowed. "Our pregnancies fail more often than succeed."

I stopped the car on the dirt road. "You've lost babies?"

She nodded her head. Tears welled in the blue pools of her eyes.

"I'm sorry. Ask me to hug you."

She shook her head.

Stubborn woman. She was almost as determined as me. I shoved the car into drive and roared the rest of the way to Arrow's house. If she wouldn't let me hug her, maybe my wolf could offer her comfort. I parked the car and jerked my t-shirt over my head. Briana's gaze landed on my bare chest. Her scent grew stronger.

"What are you doing?" she gasped.

"Shifting. I'm a wolf shifter."

"With me in the truck?" She gawked at the enclosed space. "You won't fit."

"I'll fit. I've done it before."

My blood heated with anticipation as I toed off my shoes and wriggled out of my jeans. Briana averted her gaze, but she didn't open the door and run from me. My wolf leaped at the chance to shift for his mate. One second my naked butt was on the car seat, the next, my tail wagged for Briana. A whine left my throat. Briana turned back to me.

"You should stop stripping in my presence, Sledge."

I grinned with my wolf teeth.

"Are you laughing at me in wolf form?" Her lips quirked.

I laid on the bench seat and placed my head on my paws and gave her my best puppy dog eyes. She stroked a hand from the tip of my snout, between my eyes, over the back of my head and down my back. I rumbled in pleasure with her soft touch.

"You are quite magnificent as a wolf." She stroked my fur again. "Don't let it go to your big head though."

I wriggled closer. Her hand now made its way further down my back. I wriggled closer again until my nose touched her thigh. She didn't push me away, so I laid my head in her lap. Briana didn't pause her soft caresses. My wolf rolled his eyes back in his head with pleasure. *You and me both, buddy.*

She cradled my head with both hands. I crawled onto Briana's lap and licked her face. She giggled. I licked her cheek again.

"Stop it, you overgrown puppy." She giggled again.

I slapped my tail with glee and continued licking her face. She wrapped her arms around me and hugged me.

I stopped licking her face so she could enjoy the comfort of my thick fur. Wetness slipped from her eyes onto my fur. I nuzzled her face and licked the saltiness from her cheeks.

"Oh, Sledge," she whispered, cupping my wolf face again and staring into my eyes. "What am I going to do with you?"

I butted my head against her forehead. Her hands glowed with her power. I rolled over in her lap. Her palms slithered through the softer fur of my underbelly. Over my heart. The power in her palms hummed. I didn't care how she claimed me. Me and my wolf were one and the same. If she marked one, she marked us both. My tail swished across the seat.

She shook her head and removed her hands. "Sneaky wolf."

I let out a whine.

A tap sounded on the window next to Briana's head. Saoirse and Arrow peered in through the glass. Arrow laughed. Saoirse grinned. If I had hands, I'd flip them off. I scrambled to my paws. Saoirse opened the car door.

"What's going on in here? Are you getting friendly with a wolf, Briana?" Saoirse asked.

Briana clambered from the truck and brushed my wolf fur from her dress. She firmed her lips.

"Don't worry. I can't resist petting Arrow in his wolf form either." She wrapped an arm around Briana's and led her toward the house.

I leaped from the truck and landed at Arrow's feet.

"I'm going for a run with Sledge," Arrow called out. "Stay here with Briana until we get back."

"We'll be fine here." Saoirse waved.

The women disappeared inside the house.

"Dude," Arrow said. "That was the funniest shit I've seen in a long time."

I curled my lips and snarled at my friend.

Arrow laughed and stripped his clothes. "Let's go. I think you could do with a run after that display."

I snapped at Arrow's legs. He changed in a flash of golden fur. We rolled in the dirt driveway in a play fight before running into the forest. I'd never live this down with Arrow.

After our run, I left Arrow's house and returned home to take my frustration out on the fallen tree. My muscles burned with each swing of the axe. The loud swish and solid thump a rhythm to my churning emotions. Sweat beaded my back and chest. I filled the wheelbarrow and wheeled it over to the woodshed throwing the split timber inside. I returned to the tree and swung again.

Briana's alluring scent flitted across the cool winter breeze. I kept swinging. I'd told Arrow to tell her I'd pick her up. *Why couldn't she wait for me?*

She perched on the end of the fallen tree and popped a berry in her mouth. I swung the axe making the log bounce and Briana with it.

"Why didn't you wait for me to pick you up?" I grumbled. I guess chopping the wood hadn't helped my mood.

"'Twas a lovely evening for a walk." She held up her hand. "And I found these delicious berries." She popped another one in her mouth.

I wanted to put something else in her mouth.

"How do you know they're not poisonous?"

She rolled her shoulders. "I'd survive if they were."

I slammed the axe into the tree so hard the blade stuck. "Damn it, Bree, be more careful."

"Are you worried about me?" She tossed the berries in her mouth.

I glowered at her unconcerned attitude.

"Are you provoking me, sweetheart?"

She clutched her stomach and fell to the ground with a loud groan. I rushed to her side.

"Bree?" I thrust my hands out, but she rolled away and groaned more. "What can I do? Should I get Saoirse? How can I help you?"

She laughed. "Maybe I am provoking you. Your little trick earlier almost had me. You deserved payback."

I wanted to kiss her senseless and exact another form of payback. A growl rumbled from my throat. I clenched my fingers into tight fists to stop from grabbing for her. Briana's scent ripened. She wriggled on the ground sending her short dress higher to only just covering her backside after her acting. I lowered my head to above her stomach and inhaled. She sunk a hand into my hair.

"Dia," she moaned as her skin exploded into goosebumps.

Provoke me she had.

"You want my tongue on you, don't you, Bree?"

She dropped her head back against the log. I shuffled lower until my warm breath gusted over her naked thighs.

"You smell so good," I said.

Her fingers dug into my hair harder.

"I want to lick you." I peered up the length of her body. "Shove my tongue inside you."

Her face flushed as her chest heaved and her nipples poked against her dress.

"You've been thinking about me making you scream in pleasure all day, haven't you?"

She met my lust-filled gaze and bit her lip.

"Let me give it to you."

She jerked on my hair until my face was level with hers.

"Ask me to touch you."

She parted her lips and breathed out. "No."

"I can scent your need, Bree. Let me take care of my mates needs."

Her fingers softened in my hair. Almost a caress. My skin vibrated this close to her. Her scent grew riper. More mouth watering.

"Touch yourself," I demanded.

Her eyes blazed back from her face all defiant. She'd say no yet again. But her hand slid from my hair, down my chest, it paused over my heart for a second before her hand dropped to her body. My breath faltered in my lungs. I watched her hand slide down her heaving chest to her stomach and the hem of her short dress. I couldn't tear my gaze away from her fingers.

"Do it," I encouraged her.

Her fingers disappeared under her dress. Damn, I wanted to rip it from her body and watch every stroke her fingers placed on herself. But the scent of her arousal was enough. The twitch of her body as she worked herself to orgasm was enough. For now. At least I was taking care of her the best I could.

"You'd love my thicker fingers in you."

She moaned. Her legs quivered.

"You'd love my tongue flicking your clit."

Her back bowed off the ground until her chest almost grazed mine. Just a fraction more I almost demanded but bit it back.

Instead, I said, "You'd love my cock pounding into you."

She came with a tiny gasp, almost as though she didn't want to, but she needed the release. Hell, I needed a release too. I was harder than ever watching her bring herself to orgasm. She slid her fingers from under her dress. They were shiny with her arousal. I wanted to lick them clean. But her hand shook as it travelled up her body to her hair. Her satiated expression had a look of bewilderment like she couldn't believe she'd given into her body's needs with me. She brushed her strands back, a flower fell into her palm.

"One day you will ask me to touch you," I said through my ragged breathing.

"Perhaps." She gave me a tiny smile.

"Will you touch me instead?" I cupped my hard cock.

She laughed and placed the flower in my palm. "Sneaky wolf. You can touch yourself too."

I lifted an eyebrow about to give her a show. One that would land all over her. At least she would be marked with my scent then but she scrambled out from under me and ran to the back door of the hotel. She may as well have given me a green light. Running from a wolf was like foreplay from my mate. My cock ached inside my jeans. I slid my zipper down and relieved some of the pressure. I shoved the bloom from Briana's hair to my nose and inhaled the scent that was unique to my mate. My body shuddered. I imagined she watched me from the window. I gathered the flower into my fist against my cock and stroked myself to release. Some of the pent-up tension left as I spurted onto Briana's flower in my palm as I longed to do with her.

I sat outside until the darkness of the night chilled my bones, then I walked into the hotel. Briana's scent coated every inch of air. I stripped my clothes and changed into my wolf then laid outside Briana's door where I'd spend the night. Her guardian.

Her mate.

One day soon.

I wouldn't give up until she gave in to the inevitable. Her body wanted mine. Her power wanted me, and her mind was halfway there.

Soon. Very soon. She'd be with me.

CHAPTER TEN
BRIANA

"S HITE," I CRIED, TRIPPING over the big black wolf lying in the doorway.

I landed with a thud on the floor. Sledge's wolf was over me in an instant, licking my face. I laughed at the absolute absurdity of the notion he'd slept in front of my door all night.

"Sledge." I giggled.

His thick tail wagged and thumped the floor.

We wriggled and embraced like two lovers. If I'd given in to him last night, we would have been lovers. If I'd watched him touch himself, I would have taken him for me. We'd probably be curled up in bed together instead of me waking alone, but I wasn't alone. Sledge was here for me. Could I let him in instead of keeping him at arm's length?

"Stop," I said between giggles.

Sledge sat with a start and tilted his head.

I dipped my chin to my knees and studied him. Last night I'd almost asked him to touch me. To take over from my fingers and make me scream like he promised. I wanted him. Even liked him. *Why couldn't I let my fear go and be happy?*

The wolf whined.

I sighed and patted his head. His eyes drooped in delight. I shifted closer so drawn to him I wasn't sure I could deny our connection much longer. A loud beeping rang through the hotel. Sledge shifted in an instant. His naked, and delicious muscular form on display, but he ran through the hotel leaving me with nothing but a glimpse of his bare butt. I brushed a hand to my warm cheeks and clenched my legs against the surge of desire from just one glimpse of the man naked.

He set my heart racing and my body on overdrive. Imagine what he'd do if he touched me?

Sledge returned dressed in a navy-blue uniform. He was even sexier in a uniform.

"I must go. There's a fire," he said all teasing humor gone from his voice.

"Fire?" My breathing grew shallower.

Sledge squatted. "It's a building fire. Arrow's dropping Saoirse here before we head out on the fire truck. Can you watch out for your sister while Arrow's busy?"

"Fire?" My vision turned hazy.

"Bree, focus. The fire's not here. It won't hurt you."

I blinked rapidly. Flames and burning filled my nightmares.

"I can't." I shuddered.

Sledge stood and stomped off. He returned and shoved something into my arms.

"This little fella needs you to look after him. So does your sister."

I shot my gaze to the bundle in my arms. The koala stared at me with its dark eyes. My heart melted. My fear seeped away with the warmth of the small animal nestled against my breast like a baby.

"I have to go." Sledge stood. "Briana, look at me."

I jerked my gaze to his face.

"You can do this."

I nodded.

"When I get back, you're either asking me to hug you or telling me why fire freaks you out. You need to face your fears."

I shook my head.

"Not negotiable, Bree. It's one or the other. You decide."

Sledge stomped out of the house in his heavy black boots. I swallowed the lump in my throat. He was right, I'd let my fears fester and go untouched, but it was easy in the Summer Court. The only fire in the Fae Kingdom was from Father's and Lorcan's power and there was never a question in my mind the fire would harm me. My father and brother would never hurt me. I missed them so. *How much did Saoirse miss them when she'd been on Earth a lot longer than me?*

The front door swung open, and Saoirse walked in. I sighed in relief at the sight of her and her rounded stomach.

"Why are you sitting on the floor holding a koala?" Saoirse asked.

I staggered to my feet, holding the small animal with care.

"I'm watching it while Sledge is busy."

Saoirse slumped onto the couch and plonked her feet on the cushions. I sat beside her juggling the koala in one hand and rearranging the cushions behind me in the other.

"Are you all right?" she asked.

"I miss home and everyone."

"Me too." She sighed. "I'm glad you're here."

"Do you ever think about taking Arrow to the Summer Court and living there?"

She brushed her long hair away from her shoulders. "My life is here now with my mate, but I wish I could at least visit home."

"Go back to the old ways?"

"Aye. The Trappers have been long vanished. As far as we can ascertain, we have not seen them since the burnings after Donagh went on his rampage and Father and Lorcan took the palace guards to destroy the Trappers."

My stomach flipped at the mention of my former mate's name.

"Do you miss him?" she asked.

"Aye. He was a worthy mate."

"'Twas so long ago I can scarcely remember his face," Saoirse said.

"I remember." I recalled every inch of his face, the way his eyes lit with hunger and love when he looked at me, the touch of my hands on his skin. The burn of my mark to his chest.

"Of course, you do." Saoirse pouted. "I remember how heartbroken you were after the burnings and nothing I could do helped you."

Those days were so blurry. Full of pain. I tilted my head to the side as I tried to recall Saoirse during that time. Nothing came rushing into my mind. "I don't remember you trying to help."

"No. You were beside yourself with grief, you lost your mate, you lost—"

"Don't say her name. I can't bear to hear it. Please."

"I'm sorry, Briana. I truly am. She was the image of you and our family." Her eyes welled with tears.

A tear slipped onto my cheek. It broke my heart into a million pieces. It'd never heal from the loss of my daughter.

"Our family hasn't been the same since we lost her." She caressed her stomach. "I used to wish you'd have another baby to help you heal."

"They weren't meant to be." I stood and walked into the kitchen.

Saoirse followed me.

I placed the koala in the crate. "Are you hungry?"

"I'm always hungry." She laughed.

"Growing a baby will do that to you." I opened the refrigerator. "There's Arrow's blueberry pie."

"Yes, give it to me." She clapped her hands.

We settled at the table with pieces of pie.

"You realize the birth will be difficult," I said.

"Aye. I've seen Mother give birth enough times."

I smiled. "Mother and Father truly love each other."

Saoirse screwed up her nose. "How is it she still has a heat, and you don't?"

I shrugged. I wasn't telling anyone my secret. It was bad enough Lorcan knew what I did to stop my heat. If my other siblings found out, they wouldn't be happy I hadn't shared my secret with them.

"How do you cope with Arrow fighting fires?" I asked.

Saoirse frowned and narrowed her eyes. She ate another piece of the pie. "Fires don't bother me as much as they do you. Are you worried about Sledge?"

I swallowed the piece of pie in a rush, making my eyes water.

"I knew it." She dropped her fork on the dinner table with a clatter. "You and Sledge are getting it on."

"We are not." I tucked my arms over my chest. We'd almost got it on as she so eloquently said last night. But what we did sent warmth to my cheeks.

"No, you're not. You wouldn't be this uptight if you were getting sexed up by a wolf shifter. Let me tell you, they're amazing in bed. The way they like to bite ..." She trailed off, her eyes hazing over with lust.

"Shite, Saoirse, I don't want to hear about your sex life with your mate."

She puffed out a breath. "You're the only one I have to talk to."

"Fine." I sighed.

"There are a few times where I've almost passed out."

"What?" I gasped.

"We're immortals, so that sort of thing shouldn't happen, but when he spins me around and takes me from behind and buries his teeth in my neck, oh, everything turns hazy and intense. And then..."

For the next few hours, I listened to Saoirse tell me every detail of hers and Arrow's sex life. I'd overheard enough living with them to appreciate how good they were together, but hearing her talk about it ... Shite, I huffed out a breath thinking about Sledge doing the things she talked about to me.

We were so engrossed in our talk we didn't notice Sledge and Arrow return until Sledge cleared his throat at the end of one of Saoirse's descriptions.

"What are you girls talking about?" Sledge raised an eyebrow.

"Careful, Sledge, you might feel inadequate if you knew." I raised an eyebrow back.

He scoffed.

Arrow pushed past Sledge into the kitchen and hauled Saoirse from her chair to plant a passionate kiss on her lips. They parted lips and Arrow tugged her hand. "Let's go."

Saoirse giggled. "I'll see you tomorrow, Briana." Arrow urged her to the front door. "Sledge." She nodded as she passed him.

Sledge shook his head and watched them leave.

I took the opportunity to study his soot-covered face and thank goodness unharmed body. The heat of

Saoirse's sex talk lingered in my body, but the mere presence of Sledge sent me into overdrive.

Sledge inhaled and turned his head my way. "She's quite descriptive."

"Aye." I swallowed. "You're uninjured?"

He patted his muscular arms and chest, down to his abs and thick thighs. "Yeah, I think so. Unless you want to check for yourself?"

Dia, I wished it were my hands checking him for injuries.

His finger flicked open the buttons on his shirt revealing his unharmed six-pack stomach. I wet my lips. His fingers dropped to his pants button. Moisture flooded my core. He popped the button open and slid the zipper down. I snapped my gaze away from the tempting sight.

Sledge chuckled. "I'm having a shower, then we're having our talk or hug. Whichever you've decided."

Shite. I'd forgotten about his demands. I swung my gaze his way in time to watch his shirt slip off his back as he strode out of the kitchen.

To feel a hug from Sledge would set my body into a tangle of need and want. If I let him that close, then I'd ask him to touch me in the ways he wanted to make me scream. In the ways, I'd overheard Arrow make Saoirse scream.

How much pleasure would it take to make me scream?

I longed to find out. To experience the intensity and highest highs of ecstasy, but if I let it happen once, I'd never let him go.

A talk it was then.

Icy fear slid along my veins. I'd avoided talking about the night for so long. My family never pressured me into discussing it with them. They'd suffered the loss too. The grief. The agony of losing loved ones, but not one of them understood the extent of my loss. Father had done his best to make sure none of his children ever did again by locking us inside the Summer Court. Only his children had learned we could unlock the veil with our royal powers and slip through undetected. We could venture to Earth for a short time, but we'd never stay.

CHAPTER ELEVEN

BRIANA

S LEDGE RETURNED FROM HIS shower, damp and delicious looking, but the nerves churning my stomach overrode his appeal. I hadn't even moved from the kitchen table. He slapped together a plate of food and sat opposite me.

"I suppose I'm not getting my hug?" He chomped on his food.

With a slight shake of my head, I picked up the glass of orange juice he'd placed on the table for me and gulped half the contents.

"Has Saoirse told you about the burnings at the stake that happened in the seventeen hundreds?"

His eyebrows rose. "As in like the Salem burnings in freaking ancient times?"

"Medieval times. Salem is the most referred to by humans today but there were other even more vicious trials."

"How old are you?"

"Five hundred and eighteen." I wiped the condensation on the glass.

"Shit." He scraped a forkful of food into his mouth, then signaled with his fork for me to continue.

"We used to frequent Earth before then. I quite enjoyed this realm." I pressed a hand on my chest. Earth was where I'd met my first mate. I'd always have fond memories of that time, but not what happened after. "Many Fae even lived on Earth. My mother's family lived in Ireland."

I paused to swallow the emotions thickening my throat, remembering the family I'd lost.

"Over time, humans wanted the Fae powers. They feared what we could do and what they couldn't do. The Trappers started small, picking us off in remote regions. A missing Fae here or there. Before we realized they possessed the means to subdue us and negate our powers, we'd lost many Fae."

"How many?" Sledge swiped his half-finished plate to the side.

"Thousands, perhaps more. We didn't keep track of the Fae numbers on Earth."

I shifted my gaze to the window and the call of nature outside.

Sledge shoved back his chair. "Let's finish this outside."

I followed him outside to the garden, and we settled on the half chopped fallen tree. I touched a hand onto the rough bark. My powers wanted to heal the tree. Give it back its life. Make it grow and flourish once more, but it was too late for the tree. It was too late for me to heal.

"The Fae royals have immense power over all forces."

"You do?"

"Except the females have a lesser power over all the forces and only a tremendous power over one force."

"Seems a bit unfair."

"Aye," I agreed. "Father wields the greatest power of all, but he's the king, 'tis expected of him."

Sledge's eyes never strayed from my face, but I couldn't look at him. I kept my gaze on the dead tree. So many died. The fire. The screams. I rubbed my wrists. My breathing fastened.

"What happened to your wrists, Bree?" Sledge asked.

"We, my grandparents, Mother, and sister Aislinn, we ... we went to Earth to save Mother's family, but we were too late."

"Fuck." He held his palms out. "The Trappers?"

I lay my wrists in his hands wanting his calming touch. The lingering effects of my capture eased in his warm embrace.

"They caught us too. The Trappers were sly. They'd glamoured themselves. Ironic since they were killing us for our powers and yet they'd forced witches into glamouring them, we later discovered." I raised my gaze to Sledge's face. Not his eyes. A place between his mouth and nose. A safe place. "They placed magical iron bands on our wrists so we couldn't use our powers to help anyone, let alone ourselves or each other."

"Then what happened?"

Tears dripped from my eyelashes of their own accord. "They tied us to stakes upon pyres of wood and set us on fire."

Sledge sucked in a rough breath.

"Grandmother, the Queen, was the first they set alight. Grandfather, the King, was next. It broke him watching his mate die. He didn't fight, just accepted his death. My mother's parents were next." I swallowed the pain. "They made us watch as one by one they burned us to death waiting for some insane notion that burning us alive would release our powers to them."

"Your mother and Aislinn?"

"Mother was on fire when Father rescued her. They burned her severely but she lived. Her wounds healed with time and our Spring of Life. 'Twas a long time before she spoke again. The smoke injured her lungs too. They set Aislinn and me on fire as Father, Lorcan and Saoirse appeared to save us. She suffered burns to her feet before Lorcan rescued her."

"And you?" His warm hands twitched under my wrists, but he didn't move his fingers or attempt to touch me in any other way.

"I was the same. Burns to my feet before Saoirse rescued me."

Sledge let out a long breath. "Explains your freak out over fires."

I stared off into the darkness of the night. My breath puffed out in clouds of white smoky frost. If I was human, I'd be cold, and the flimsy dress would be no protection. If I was human, I'd want the warmth of a fire.

"What else happened?" Sledge asked.

"Nothing."

"Liar. Tell me it all, Bree. You need to let it out."

I stood in a flourish, my power surged, and the fallen tree burst into life with fresh green leaves.

"Feel better?" He cocked an eyebrow.

"No," I whispered. I'd felt better with my wrists in his hands. "You want to know it all. Fine. I'll tell you. Then you'll understand why I'll never accept another mate."

"You had a mate?"

"Aye, his name was Donagh. We met, and we mated in the way of the Fae. We weren't fated but we chose each other and we were happy." I tugged my dress down my chest. My mating mark was a white scar now my mate was dead, but the lines were still visible. "He died."

"How did he die?"

My power rippled. The ground burst into a field of yellow daffodils.

"After we arrived back at the Summer Court, injured and broken from the burnings, I learned Donagh had left for Earth to rescue me. He was a warrior. If I hadn't raced off with Mother to help rescue her parents, he wouldn't have left the Summer Court."

Sledge opened his mouth.

I sliced my fist through the air, smothering his face with a branch.

"We had a daughter. A beautiful girl with long white hair and a sweet nature. She loved animals and could communicate with them. She was everything to us." I swiped my hand across my cheek, not surprised to find

I was crying. "I was a mess after watching, well, you understand, all I saw was flames and death. All I smelled was burning flesh. All I heard were the screams of my family.

"Donagh left the Summer Court and killed the remaining Trappers in my mother's home village where I'd almost died. He didn't stop there though. He kept cleaving heads of any Trapper he found. Our daughter followed him. Nobody knew until it was too late."

Sledge wriggled under the branch. I forced more power into the leaves to keep them and him in place. He wanted to know it all. Damn him, he'd hear it all without interrupting otherwise I'd never get it out.

"Deirdre fit her name. Fearsome one. She took after her father. But she was young, impetuous. She had no fighting skills. The Trappers captured her and burned her at the stake. Donagh discovered her body. I was told by Lorcan, who was with Father and the King's guard. They had at last caught up to him. Lorcan couldn't get Donagh to return to me. Our daughter's death broke him. He went off on his own again. I returned to Earth with Lorcan only to find the Trappers had burned Donagh at the stake too."

I pressed both fists to my eyes as though I could erase the image from my mind. But I couldn't. They forever scarred it in my memories.

"So, Sledge, you wanted to know the entire story. There it is. My mate, my daughter, dead. If not for me, they'd both be alive still and I wouldn't have their ashes on my hands."

Sledge ripped the branch from his face with a sudden heave of strength. "Bree." He croaked out my name.

"No," I snapped. "I can't have you as my mate for I'd forever be wondering if your future death and our future children's deaths would be my fault."

"It wasn't your fault." He stood as though he was declaring an important truth.

"Wasn't it?" I swept my hand across the garden dragging the flowers back into the ground and the leaves into nothing. The tree was nothing now. It shouldn't have leaves. Like I shouldn't have anything either.

"No," he said with conviction. "You need to stop blaming yourself for their deaths. They made their choices. You didn't force them to go to Earth and you didn't tell Donagh to hunt the Trappers. You didn't ask your daughter to follow your mate. They did it all themselves. It doesn't make it any better, but it *wasn't your fault*."

"Fault or no, their deaths are mine."

"Their deaths aren't yours. They are yours. Your mate and daughter live on in you and your memories. Stop blaming yourself and start remembering all the good times you had together."

A small smile ghosted across my lips. "We had good times."

"See." He stepped closer to me. "Tell me your favorite thing about your mate."

I raised my eyebrows. This man, who wanted me for himself, asked me to tell him about my former mate. Dia, he kept surprising me.

"He would travel to anywhere on Earth and pick me the freshest blueberries. We have gormberries in the Summer Court which are similar but the blueberries of Earth taste a tad different. Sweeter somehow. I prefer Earth blueberries. All Fae do."

Sledge laughed. "You and Saoirse and your blueberries."

I shrugged. "They're delicious."

"What about Deirdre? What was your favorite thing about your daughter?"

"Her smile," I said without thinking. "She smiled with the pure innocence of a Fae child who loved life."

"Remember the blueberries and her smile. Not the other stuff. Celebrate their lives instead of mourning them."

I placed a hand to Sledge's cheek. "You're such a kind man."

"Wolf shifter, sweet thing." He winked.

I laughed. "And then you ruin it."

"I ruined nothing." He pouted.

I dropped my hand. No, he ruined nothing. He always chose the right moment when I needed his light humor. "Thank you for listening but it changes nothing for us."

"Stop fighting, Bree."

"I can't. If I stop fighting, what do I have left?" I walked across the garden to the back door.

"Me," Sledge whispered.

I kept walking into the house and to my bedroom. If I had Sledge and gave in to the intense need to have him as my mate, then what? In the quietness of my lone bedroom, I felt truly alone. I'd spent all my emotions after I confessed my past. I padded into the connecting bathroom and showered, hoping to revive myself, but all the scorching water did was drain me further. Stepping out of the steamy haze, I dried and slid on the plush robe.

A scratch sounded on my bedroom door. I crossed the small space and opened the door. Sledge's big black wolf greeted me with a whine.

"Sledge, I'm tired. I just want to go to bed."

The wolf strutted into my room and sprung on my bed.

I crossed my arms. "I sleep naked."

The wolf ducked his head under his paws.

I couldn't help but laugh and shimmy closer to the bed. "Fine. But you stay on top of the covers and no shifting."

He thumped his tail.

"No peeking." I slid off the robe, dropped it on the chair, and climbed the platform to the bed. I slithered under the soft sheets and thick blanket. "Okay, you can look now."

The wolf raised his head and crawled closer with his tail wagging. He laid by my side with the barest of touches of his snout on my shoulder. I slid my hand into his thick fur, rolled over, and wrapped my arm around his enormous size.

"I guess you're getting your talk and hug tonight."

He yipped and licked my face.

I shook my head. Sneaky wolf, always getting his way. If I wasn't careful, he'd get what he wanted, every single one of them, including me claiming him as my mate.

CHAPTER TWELVE

SLEDGE

"**Q**UICKER, JONATHON," I YELLED. "The fire won't wait for you to be ready."

Jonathon unwound the length of the fire hose from the clean truck.

"Dean, get in there and help," I snapped. "Hustle, hustle."

Arrow folded his arms over his chest and quirked his lip.

"Don't say a thing," I grumbled.

Arrow drummed his fingers on his arm and raised an eyebrow saying it all with his actions instead of words.

I faced him. "Why didn't you tell me about the Trappers?"

"Briana told you?" He unfolded his arms.

"Yeah, she told me her horror story. What I can't understand is why you didn't tell me."

"It wasn't my story to tell." He turned his attention to Jonathon and Dean unwinding the hose from the fire truck. "Good job, guys. Take the hose to the small building over there and get ready."

Jonathon and Dean scurried across the small paddock to our firefighting training building.

"Look," Arrow said. "I saw Saoirse's memories. The burnings were a living hell, but the aftereffects were worse."

"A warning would've at least been good."

"How can you warn someone about the past?" He stroked his jaw.

I walked to the truck and rested against the cool metal. "She lost her mate and her child."

"Yeah." His voice came out sad as though he'd felt the loss too.

"Did you see them in Saoirse's memories?"

"I did." Arrow sat on the step. "Their kid was super cute."

"And her mate?"

"He was a redhead with a bit of a temper and impulse control issues."

Jonathon and Dean battled the imaginary blaze in the building. More battling with the hose than anything. The pair needed to work out more, build muscle and strength for the force in the water coming through the thick hose.

"But they loved each other," I said, saying the one thing Arrow was reluctant to tell me.

"Yeah, they did." He kept his gaze on the imaginary fire battle.

"I never stood a chance, did I?"

"I'm going to sound like a girl." He stroked a hand through his hair. "After seeing Saoirse's memories, I would have said no. But after seeing you two together, I'd say yes. Briana looks at you the way Saoirse looks at me."

"What, like I'm a juicy blueberry?"

Arrow laughed. "The number of blueberries she eats now."

"Her stomach looks like a giant blueberry."

He laughed harder.

"What if the baby comes out blue?" I asked.

"He could come out any color and I wouldn't care so long as he's healthy."

I slapped him on the shoulder. "He'll be fine."

"Saoirse still worries."

"And you?"

"Shit, Sledge, we're turning into a pair of girls. I worry too. It's hard not to."

"Yeah." I slammed a fist into my palm. "How about we hit the gym after here?"

"Hell, yeah. Mom is with Saoirse and Briana is too. I can stay out longer."

"Pussy whipped." I whipped my hand in the air and made a whipping noise.

"The best way to be when it's your mate's pussy." Arrow laughed and strode over to our newest recruits.

I kicked the grass. Perhaps it was best if I let him deal with the training. I was in no mood to train newbies. No mood for anything but my mate and feeling her delicate arms around my body again. Even in wolf form. The smug bastard rumbled with pleasure he'd gotten a hug and I didn't. Stupid wolf. We were one and the same. I climbed into the truck and shut my eyes. A brief nap might put me in a better mood.

Sometime later, I woke to Arrow's grinning face. Another smug bastard. My hackles were already rising. I scraped a hand over my eyes and clambered from the truck. I needed to reign in my frustration.

"How'd you guys go?"

"Awesome." Dean grinned.

"Yeah, that was cool," Jonathon said.

"You'll need to muscle up more." I eyed their slim frames. They had wolf shifter strength, but they needed muscular strength to control the fire hose. "We're heading to the gym if you want to join us."

"For sure." Dean clambered into the fire truck followed by Arrow.

"What about you, Jonathon?"

"I'm supposed to meet up with Clara." He glanced at the ground.

"How is your new mate?" I slung an arm over his shoulders. "Are you as whipped as Arrow?"

"Good, but she wants to wait for me to claim her until her friend finds her mate." He shrugged. "It's this ridiculous pact they made."

"You mean Eloise?"

"Yep. I don't think Clara wants to leave her living in the house alone."

"That sucks for you." I grimaced, imagining Briana not living with me.

"Tell me about it. I can't believe I'm so lucky to find my mate already and now I must wait." He whined.

"Eloise would be all right living by herself. The entire town looks out for everyone." I pointed out what he'd already know, having been born and raised in the Crystal Creek wolf pack.

"She's strange." His gaze skittered to the house they'd pretended to fight a fire in.

"Eloise or Clara?"

"Eloise. She says some weird shit sometimes." He ducked out from under my arm.

"Like what?"

"Don't worry about it." He opened the door of the firetruck.

"Jonathon, what does she say?" I let my Alpha wolf ripple through my voice.

He jerked. "She says it's not fair a Fae mated with the best wolf in our pack."

An inner alarm blared through my body. "What else?"

Jonathon shuffled his feet. "She ... ah ... she says stuff like being destined to reign. Whatever that means."

"Thanks for telling me."

Jonathon climbed onto the edge of the truck.

"Hey," I said. "If she says anything strange again, come tell me, okay?"

"Sure." Jonathon opened the door and retreated into the truck.

As if I didn't have enough to worry about with my mate unwilling to accept we were mates and figuring out a way to help her with her post-traumatic stress. Add to that, my best friend's upcoming fatherhood, and the stress around the birth of a Fae wolf shifter hybrid. Now I had to worry about Eloise more than I was after she'd hit on Arrow when he'd already marked Saoirse. If she tried anything with Arrow again, Saoirse would probably gut her with her water Katana. The comment which niggled more, was the one about being destined to reign.

What did she think she was going to reign?

Our pack had an Alpha, my father, and he was a long way from handing over the reins. Not that a female wolf shifter could be Alpha. We didn't work that way. It was always a male as Alpha.

I scraped a hand over my jaw and climbed into the truck. Arrow shot me a look, but I smiled. There was no need to add to Arrow's worries. I'd handle Eloise.

"Hey," I said to Briana as she sat at the dining table opposite me. I'd made sure Clara cooked the meals and left to give us more time together alone. "How was your day?"

"Good. I met Arrow's mother, Marianne. She's delightful. We spent most of the day organizing the spare bedroom into a nursery."

I nodded and ate a forkful of the spaghetti. "Yours is vegetarian."

"Thanks." Briana twirled her fork in the pasta and ate.

Silence descended between us. The only sounds in the kitchen were those of us eating. I finished my bowl of pasta and Briana shoved her half-eaten meal aside.

"Aren't you hungry?"

"Not really." She swallowed. "Why is there an unlit candle and a box of matches on the table?"

"Are you scared of a little flame from a candle?"

She firmed her lips but didn't answer me. My hunch that any fire at all freaked her out might be right.

"We're working on your fear tonight."

She ran her hands down the sides of her dress until her hands disappeared from my sight.

"I donna know about this." She licked her lips. Flicked her gaze to the window. A glow emanated from under the table.

"Breathe, Bree. I won't let anything hurt you. It will be one small, controlled flame. I'll light it for a minute and then you can blow it out."

She blinked rapidly as her eyes took on a glassy glaze.

I picked up the matchbox and slid it open, drawing out one red-tipped matchstick I swiped it along the side of the box. The matchstick burst into flame with a flare of stinky sulfur.

Briana gulped a lungful of air and slammed her hands on the table.

"I can't." She eyed the matchstick like the tiny flame would burn her alive.

I lit the candle quickly and shook the matchstick with a flick of my wrist to extinguish the flame. Briana rubbed her wrists in a furious motion that would strip skin if she kept it up. I laid my hands, palms up on the table. Her gaze dropped to them, and she placed her wrists in my soft embrace.

"You're doing great, sweetheart."

Her gaze slammed back to the candle and the flame.

"It's tiny. Nothing bad can happen. Nothing bad will happen to you with me around. I'm a firefighter. Fighting fires is what I do for a living. I understand how flames work. I know how to extinguish them."

The candle dripped a trail of hot wax.

"Keep breathing. Another thirty seconds and you can blow out the candle. Did I ever tell you why I became a firefighter?" I asked, hoping to distract her.

Briana shook her head.

"When I was seven, the firetruck visited the school and gave this cool demonstration. I was super impressed with everything they said and did, but what I loved the most was the force of the hose in my arms as I squirted water. The hose was like this living breathing, being, and it chose me to focus its force where it was needed. Without me, it wouldn't know where it was needed."

The timer on my phone beeped.

"Blow the flame out."

Briana puffed out a breath so quick the flame whooshed out in a rush my way.

"Good work, sweet thing."

Her pulse pounded fast in my palms, but I didn't ease it with a stroke of my thumbs as I wanted. She needed to battle the fear herself.

"Where was I? The day after the firetruck visited the school I found my first injured koala." I nodded at the crate in the corner of the kitchen. "A fire burned the koala, and he was crying in pain. I tried to reach it, but the tree it was in was tall and spindly. So, I called the fire brigade. They rushed to the koala's rescue, climbed to the top branches on their long ladder, and handed the animal to me."

"What did you do?" Briana asked.

I chuckled. "The only thing I could do. I nursed the koala until it was well enough to be released back into the forest. While everyone cheered for the firefighter up the ladder, I realized that's what I wanted to be. A firefighter so I could help anyone and anything."

Briana removed her hands from mine. I picked up our dirty plates and shoved them in the dishwasher. I strode for the door.

"Sledge, wait."

I stopped. She could command me to do anything for her and I would.

"Thank you."

I nodded. "We'll do more tomorrow night."

"Sledge." Briana shoved back her chair. "Would it be too much to ask if we did what we did last night?"

"Nothing you ask of me is too much." Even though it was too much to lie with her in bed knowing she was naked under the blankets and sheets. It was better than sleeping in my bed alone or in front of her door. "Leave the door open when you're ready for me to come in."

Bit by bit, she was cracking the door open. I wanted to take the axe from the yard and chop it to splinters. Being this close to my mate and not having her ripped me apart from the inside out. My wolf would be happy he'd feel her soft hands in his fur again. He whimpered. He knew this half-life was not a life at all.

If Briana didn't crack soon, I might crack.

CHAPTER THIRTEEN
BRIANA

A MONTH PASSED IN a quickness I never saw coming. Every minute with Sledge filled all the lonesome places. Watching him sword fight with Saoirse, then teaching him to staff fight until our breaths panted and our skin slicked with sweat. Every cheeky remark and sexual innuendo he flung my way set my body into a flare of need. So hungry for him. I was crumbling. Cracking under the lure and attraction of my mate. Thank the Summer Court I wasn't in heat otherwise I'd strip him bare and ride him the way I ached to do.

Confessing my past relieved a tremendous burden from my essence, like I could at last breathe again. The hurt, pain, and loss were still there, they always would be, but now they were the smaller parts of my memories. Instead, I now remembered my mate and daughter with the love and affection we shared. All the good times as Sledge said. I even started talking with Saoirse about them, much to her surprise, but she was a wonderful sister and didn't ask where my sudden change of heart appeared from. It was obvious Sledge was the reason.

Even our evening ritual with the candle was a moment I cherished with Sledge. The small flame no longer bothered me with Sledge telling me details of his life. I was desperate to learn more about him and he didn't disappoint. He never did. He went out of his way to please me and give me whatever I asked for.

His wolf, who was fierce looking, was the cuddliest of creatures alive with me. He warmed my heart with his gentleness. His wolf soothed me in ways the man couldn't. He took the pressure off wanting to be with my mate and the knowledge that if we crossed the line into sleeping together as man and woman, then there'd be no going back. He would claim me and I him.

My power crackled in my hands. It was harder and harder to keep from marking Sledge as mine. He was. Not in every way yet.

Yet.

There was the word I never thought I'd say.

I shimmied into the lush green dress decorated with a pastel pink overlay and a long flowing skirt. Another of Arrow's creations. Not that anyone other than me and Saoirse knew Arrow made our dresses. The town thought we magicked them. If only that were possible. I stepped out of my bedroom to find Sledge waiting for me dressed in a suit and tie.

"My, you are handsome," slipped out of my mouth uncensored.

Sledge grinned. "Scrub up okay, do I, sweet thing?"

"More than okay." I ran a hand down his tie.

Sledge's eyes widened at my intimate touch.

"I didn't realize your sister's thirteenth birthday was a formal occasion. I don't possess any formal dresses to wear." *Why hadn't Arrow made me a formal dress for tonight?* Saoirse didn't have a formal dress either.

"You look beautiful. Like a princess. Although I prefer you in the short dresses so I can see your sexy legs."

I chuckled. "I am a princess."

"Yeah, your flower crown is a dead giveaway." He grinned. "We should go. Dad will have my balls if I'm late."

"We can't have that." I walked to the door and flung a look over my shoulder. "I might want to use them one day soon."

Without missing a step after my admission, I kept walking outside. Sledge didn't walk beside me. I turned around to find Sledge standing stock still in the house.

"Sledge, let's go."

He wrenched the door shut behind him and stalked toward me. His eyes glowed in the gathering twilight of the spring evening.

"Did I hear you right?"

I batted my eyelashes. "Did you?"

"Bree," he groaned. "Don't toy with me. I'm living with a constant hard-on for you and my hand isn't cutting it anymore."

My gaze slid to his hands. I'd like to watch him pleasure himself. I wish I had that day I'd left him in the garden. Even more, I'd like to watch him pleasure me.

Music blared from the town square.

"Shit," Sledge said. "We have to go." He stomped off down the sidewalk.

I trotted along beside him and flicked him a wary gaze. *Did my one small comment stun him that much?* He was adamant we were mates. *If I was giving in to him, was it any surprise?*

The crowd of wolf shifters milled around the town square where they'd set up rows of long tables and strands of twinkling fairy lights. A band played from the gazebo where a bunch of teenagers danced. No doubt, Heidi's friends. Would they hate me too the same as Heidi? They looked happy and carefree. Oh, to be young again without the weight of past haunts. I shut the thought down. This was a party, and it was time I let myself enjoy life again. Even if the guest of honor might still hate me for using my powers on her.

Sledge took us straight to the birthday girl sitting on a throne-like chair decorated in bright yellow balloons.

"Happy birthday, sis." Sledge gave Heidi a rub on her head.

I rolled my eyes. As if she wanted to be treated like a little kid on this momentous occasion. I swept in front of Sledge.

"Happy birthday, young woman." I dipped a curtsy hoping to mend the hurt I'd caused with our first meeting. "May this day be the beginning of great things." I waved my hand across the ground drawing a carpet of white daisies to spring up under her feet.

Heidi clapped her hands.

Seemed she at least liked my powers now. I plucked the daisies and fashioned a daisy chain then placed the ring on top of her head. "There, now you're a princess too on your birthday."

"Thank you." She beamed.

I returned her smile. This was how I wished meeting Sledge's sister first went.

Sledge fished in his pocket and handed her a small box. Heidi opened the box with a huge grin on her youthful face. She twirled the sparkling gold chain.

"Thanks, Sledge." She vaulted out of the chair and hugged him. "I'll wear it tomorrow after our hunt tonight."

Sledge ruffled her hair. "I'm looking forward to teaching you a few new tricks."

Heidi laughed. "If you can keep up with me now you're getting older."

Sledge raised his brow. "Older? Why you little punk? I'll show you who's faster tonight."

"Children," Kelly said walking up to us with Ray. "There will be no racing tonight. The hunt will be organized and dignified."

Sledge snorted.

I placed a hand to my mouth and covered my laugh. Sledge would never be dignified.

"It's a pleasure to see you here," Ray said.

"Thank you for your hospitality."

"May I have a word with you alone?" Ray asked.

"Of course."

We walked away from the group to a quiet spot near the border of the town square between two dark buildings. The shadows were dark and oppressive after the festivities of the party.

"I don't want to alarm you, but Saoirse and Arrow won't be here tonight. The shifter doctor thinks she might be close."

"So soon. She's not ready yet." Panic lanced through my body.

"Hence, he's put her on bedrest and strict instructions for no excitement," Ray said calmly.

"I should go see her." I stepped away from him.

"Wait." He reached out.

I jerked back avoiding his hand.

"Sorry," he said. "It's just, I wanted to say I'm happy to see you here with Sledge and you should stay at the party with him. There's nothing you can do for Saoirse. Arrow will tell us when she goes into labor."

"I ... ah." I was torn. My sister's welfare was the reason I was on Earth, but Sledge was the reason I'd enjoyed my time here.

"When we head out for the hunt, you can visit Saoirse then."

"True." I dipped my head and searched the crowd for Sledge. I should at least stay until they left for the hunt.

"I'm surprised with Sledge's strength," Ray said.

"In what way?" I asked. Sledge was strong with his muscles upon muscles, and then there was his wolf shifter strength.

"In not marking you straight away." He shoved his hands into his pants pockets. "Alpha wolves aren't known for going easy on marking their claim. I was lucky my mate didn't rip me a new one when I claimed her."

"Kelly would do that to you? She looks like she loves you very much."

Ray chuckled. "My mate has claws. Ones she reminds me of often. But she didn't love me when I marked her, so I was lucky she didn't use them on me."

What was he getting at? Did he think I loved Sledge? My brow furrowed. A man called out to Ray and waved him over.

"Sorry, I should get back to the party," he said.

"Aye." I waved him off.

My mind was a whirl as I slid into the crowd of wolf shifters. I should look for Sledge, but I couldn't face him with his father's words pounding in my head. In our short time together, had I fallen in love with the outrageously sweet, yet over-the-top Alpha wolf shifter? My heart thudded to every step I took through the town square. I sunk onto a seat at a table.

A prickle of unease skittered up my back. I searched the crowd to the right. Sledge stood with the woman who'd been at his house the first night I'd arrived at his hotel. What was her name? I drummed my fingers on the tabletop. Eloise. She set my hackles on the rise and I wasn't a wolf shifter. She stepped closer to Sledge and rested a hand on his huge bicep straining under the suit. My power surged, but I tamped the growing pulse to stop my palms from glowing. I didn't want to alarm the wolf shifters at the party. Or upset Heidi with my powers again.

Sledge smiled and leaned closer to Eloise.

If only I could hear like a wolf shifter. What was he whispering in her ear? Was he fooling me into thinking we were mates when he had a thing with that woman? I shook my head, clearing the haze of jealousy.

No. This was something else. Sledge wouldn't do that to me.

Eloise threw back her head and laughed.

Dia, she looked happy beside Sledge. If I gave in to Sledge, would I look that happy? Feel that happy? Experience happiness like I'd once shared with a mate. I picked up a glass of water from the table and gulped the contents.

Heidi sat in the chair to my left.

I swung from watching Sledge to Heidi, for all intents and purposes giving Sledge my back and cutting off any sight of him with another woman.

"I don't like her," Heidi said.

"Who?"

"Eloise. The new woman in town." Heidi picked up a napkin and ripped it to shreds.

"You don't like me either," I pointed out.

She tossed the napkin on the table. "She wants Sledge. Why are you letting her touch him?"

"Me?"

"You're Sledge's mate." She scowled. "You should be over there stopping her."

"I'm not his mate."

Heidi flapped her hand in front of my face. "Hello. Yes, you are. I'd much prefer him with a wolf shifter, but Eloise is blah." She pretended to gag.

"Stop acting like a child." I grabbed her arm.

She glared. "Stop acting like you don't give a damn about my brother."

"Heidi." I sighed. "There are things you don't comprehend."

"Like what?" She shoved her hands on her hips over her pretty yellow dress matching the balloons hanging around the town square.

"Like a lot of things, princess." I straightened the daisy crown on top of her head. "When you're as old as me, there are a lot of things."

"But we've always been told a mate will care for you no matter what. And we should always listen to the call of a mate." Her face softened. "I can't wait for the day I meet my mate. I'll be his princess wolf shifter and he'll be the white knight willing to do anything for me."

"You hold on to the fairy tale." I cupped her youthful face. Dia, she reminded me of my daughter at that age. So impetuous, so full of life and love.

She shook her head out of my hands.

"You can have the fairy tale too. Sledge isn't a white knight, more a black wolf, but he's your mate. He'll do anything for you." She ripped another napkin to pieces. "Fae are stupid."

I pondered her words. Sledge had done anything for me so far. That wasn't the problem. I was. And I sure wasn't stupid. Stubborn perhaps, but not stupid.

"Are you nervous about the hunt?" I asked, changing the subject. The girl didn't like me enough as it was. And this was Sledge's sister. I couldn't have that.

"No," she tried to scoff but it didn't come out.

"There's no shame in being nervous of your first time."

She lifted her gaze. "What if I mess up?"

I squeezed her hand. "You won't. And no one will expect you to be perfect your first time. What are you hunting?"

"Wild pig. Those animals are such a pest here. And they taste good." She licked her lips.

"I don't eat meat."

Heidi's mouth fell open.

I tapped her chin shut. "You'll eat the bugs. You want to save your tastebuds for the pig."

She giggled. "I don't hate you."

My lips twitched in a small smile. "I like you too." How could I not like her, she was a miniature female version of Sledge in a way.

"Do you like Sledge?"

My smile dropped. "You don't let up, do you?"

"Nope. Ma says Sledge and I take after Dad that way."

"I can see that." I scooped her shredded napkins into a pile.

"So, do you?" She persisted.

"Aye. I like your brother."

"Yes." She fist-pumped the air.

Except her fist met someone else's. I swung my head to find Sledge grinning down at me.

Heidi vaulted from the chair. "Here, take my seat."

Sledge ruffled her hair dislodging the daisy crown. I rolled my eyes.

"So, you like me, huh?" He settled beside me.

I pursed my lips. "Don't let it go to your head."

"Which head?"

I laughed despite his crudeness. "Both."

He placed his hand on the back of my chair and leaned closer to me. His warm breath sent shivers through my body and peaked my nipples under my dress.

"Too late. Both heads are massive now."

Warmth flooded my body from the inside out. My gaze dropped to his lap. Sure enough, a bulge tented the fabric of his suit.

"Damn it, why do you have to look at my junk now like you want to take a bite?"

I wet my lips. It was indeed what I wanted to do. Run my lips and tongue over his hard length. Sledge's chest rumbled, sending sparks of need straight to my core.

Somewhere in the town square, a horn blew.

Sledge forced his chair back. "It's time for the hunt. Will you be okay to head back home by yourself or do you want me to walk you?"

I blinked but couldn't take my gaze off his impressive bulge. "I'll be fine."

Sledge muttered something, but I didn't make out what it was. He strode away leaving me with the delectable view of his tight backside. Another place I wanted to lick and kiss. I brushed my hands to my hot cheeks.

The wolf shifters stripped and shifted into their wolves. With a lot of yipping and the occasional howl, they raced through the town and into the darkness of the forest. I let out a long sigh wishing I dared to make Sledge my mate.

CHAPTER FOURTEEN

BRIANA

S OMETHING WAS WRONG. IF the baying wolves hadn't warned me, then the prickle of unease skittering up and down my spine would have. The front door of Sledge's house burst open. Sledge's mom stood stark naked holding the door. Sledge rushed inside, also naked, with his naked unconscious father in his arms.

Blood. So much blood.

Crimson dripped along Sledge's arm and down his legs running rivers of claret life onto the floor. He strode into the kitchen and placed his father carefully on the table. Heidi ran inside, also naked. I rushed to my bedroom and grabbed my robe, wrapping it around the shaking girl's shoulders.

"What happened?" I slid a hand to Sledge's elbow.

"He, he, fell off a rock ledge and landed on that." Sledge pointed at the long stick sticking out of his father's chest. "Take it out, Bree, please."

"No." I stayed his hand as he grabbed for it. "You'll make it worse. Call your healer."

"We don't have a healer," he said. "We have doctors."

I sucked in a breath. Tasting the metallic tang of blood in the air and studied the branch. The limb was too close to the Alpha's heart. If I removed it without a healer present, then blood loss would overcome him. Perhaps he'd even die.

"A doctor won't help in time. You need magical assistance." I placed a hand on the limb and let my power hum into the branch to steady it from moving and doing more damage. "Don't suppose you have a Caladrius or Unicorn anywhere nearby?"

Sledge snorted. "A Unicorn, for real?"

"Aye, we have them in the Summer Court. Perhaps I should return and get some Allicorn for his wound."

"You're not going anywhere," Sledge ground out through gritted teeth, his muscles tensing under my hand.

"Wizard or witch then?"

Sledge clicked his fingers and dived for his phone on the benchtop. He punched the screen then barked into the device, "Pepper, I need urgent healing help."

A witch then. I couldn't hear her response.

"Yes, I understand, I already owe you," Sledge replied. "I'll owe you more if you bring your cute butt over to my house and help heal my father."

Cute butt?

Who was this witch and what did she mean to Sledge?

My power hummed stronger.

"We could get Saoirse here," I interrupted. "She can help slow the blood flow."

"She's on bed rest," Kelly said.

Shite. I shouldn't stress Saoirse in her condition. I understood how worried she was about her baby.

"Right." I frowned.

Sledge stepped away from us. "Pepper, please." He was silent a moment. "Yes. Okay. No. All right and thank you." He hung up the phone and ran a hand over his head, smearing blood into his hair before moving back to the table. "She'll be here soon."

I pursed my lips.

Kelly held Ray's hand between both of hers. Heidi sobbed in the corner. Sledge paced to his room and returned wearing tracksuit pants and handed a robe to his mother, then placed a towel over his father's lower body. My power hummed on the branch. Blood oozed from the wound over Ray's chest and onto the table.

The minutes stretched.

Drip. Drip. The blood rolled from the table onto the floor. Heidi's sobs grew louder. Kelly's hands tightened on her mates. Sledge stopped pacing. My power flared harder, but there was nothing I could do to stop the blood. If I disintegrated the branch, the blood would rush like a dam breaking.

Sledge's gaze met mine. He realized his father had little time left. I longed to wrap my arms around him and hug him. Comfort him in his time of need. My mate was aching, and I wasn't doing anything to soothe him.

"Bree?" he whispered.

If I let go of my hold on the branch, his father would die. If I held on, he'd have a few minutes for everyone to say goodbye.

"He doesn't have much time left," I said gently.

Kelly burst into tears.

"I'm not saying goodbye." Sledge folded his arms.

"Perhaps you should, while you can." My eyelashes felt heavy with all the emotions in the room, so I closed my eyes for a second. "I wish I had the chance to say goodbye," I whispered as I opened my eyes and zeroed my gaze on Sledge, the meaning loud and clear.

He stomped to the window overlooking the garden.

"Ray," Kelly squeaked. "Ray, I love you, you stubborn Alpha asshole. Don't you leave me. You hang on. Help is on the way."

I rolled my eyes. Not the goodbye I envisioned.

"Daddy." Heidi rushed to his side next to Kelly. "I'm sorry. I never should have tried to outrun Sledge. If it wasn't for me, you wouldn't be hurt. Daddy, wake up, please. I ... I need you to ground me."

Sledge choked on a laugh then swallowed. It'd break my heart to hear him talk to his dying father.

The front door flew open. A stunning woman with thick black hair and a streak of red streamed into the house wearing a billowing black cloak. Witches always loved to make a grand entrance.

"Out of the way, wolfies," the witch said.

Kelly and Heidi scuttled to a corner in the kitchen, hugging each other.

"Hurry, Pepper," Sledge pleaded.

"Yes, yes." She swept her hand over Ray's body and met my gaze. "A Fae princess. Are you Arrow's mate?"

"No. My sister Saoirse is."

"Oooh, two princesses."

"Pepper," Sledge snapped.

She flung her cape off her shoulders and ripped two vials from a pouch at her waist. One vial she poured on the wound, the other she tipped into Ray's mouth after holding his nose. Ray spluttered but swallowed the potion even though he wasn't conscious.

"There." She slid the empty vials back into the pouch. "You can remove the branch now."

I raised an eyebrow and let my power disintegrate the limb into nothing expecting a gush of blood from the gaping wound, but the wound appeared to be cauterized.

"Nice potions," I said. This witch exhibited phenomenal powers. I'd met only one other like her many moons ago, long before the burnings. "What line do you come from?"

She thrust her hand across Ray's body. "Pepper Woods."

I shook her hand. "Briana O'Cliergh. Woods? I could have sworn your powers were reminiscent of another line."

"And your powers?" She gripped my hand tighter.

My palm glowed as though she was testing my powers.

"Nature. Lovely." She let go of my hand and gathered up her cloak.

Sledge took it from her hands and settled it on her shoulders. "Thank you, Pepper."

Pepper patted his cheek. "You owe me two favors now."

"Tit for tat." He removed her hand from his face and flicked his gaze my way. "You witch's can never do anything just for the good of it."

"Where would be the fun in that?" She cackled. "I'll see you soon, Sledge. Briana, charming to meet a true bona fide Fae princess." She strode for the door, then paused. "Oh, those potions will keep your dad out of action for a bit I'm afraid. Sorry I didn't mention it before giving them to him." She cackled again and swooped out the door.

Kelly and Heidi rushed back to Ray's side. I stepped back and made room for Sledge to join his family. They weren't mine. I didn't belong with them at this moment. If I'd accepted Sledge's mating, then I would, but as it was, I was an outsider, and this was a private moment. I opened the back door and slipped outside, sunk to the grass and with every passing minute I let my power hum more into the beauty of nature and all its creations. Death was never my strength.

"Bree, thank you." Sledge sat on the ground by my side.

"You're welcome." A tulip popped up from the ground next to my palm.

He reached a hand for me then stopped.

"I ... ah ... shit ... I'm covered in blood." His voice cracked.

He rose with a scrabble of limbs as though he couldn't get away fast enough and disappeared into the house.

Sledge was in pain and the call to soothe my mate was too much. I followed him into the house noting the absence of his family in the kitchen. *How long had I sat outside lost in my thoughts?*

I knocked on his bedroom door. No answer. I knocked again. I took two steps down the hallway and spun back. There was a pull deep in my chest to go to Sledge. I twisted the doorknob and let myself into his bedroom. The room was all Sledge. Dark drapes hung at the window. A thick black bedspread covered his enormous bed in the center of his room with a splash of a white fur rug hanging across the end of the bed. A small beechwood desk sat next to a fireplace with a slingback chair in raw leather. The sound of running water emanated from a door to my left. He was in the shower. I should go.

Instead, I perched on the edge of his bed and passed my fingers through the fur rug. It was soothing, like the times I'd run my fingers through Sledge's wolf fur, except this fur was softer.

The bathroom door opened, and Sledge walked out in a towel. He stopped and tugged the towel tighter.

"Bree, I can't shift tonight."

"I don't want you to." I stroked the fur.

"What do you want?" He took a step closer.

"I wanted to make sure you were all right after what happened to your father. It can't have been easy seeing him injured so grievously."

He swallowed and stepped to his closet. "No, it wasn't easy and no I'm not all right."

"What can I do? You're always there for me. I want to be here for you."

He dropped his towel and yanked on a pair of boxer shorts before facing me.

Even that brief glimpse of his naked rear end sent my heart fluttering in madness. He tilted his head to the side and studied me from head to foot. Flames of heat licked along my body. Sledge's eyes grew hooded.

"You look mighty fine on my bed." His voice dipped lower.

A shiver of need danced a trail along my body as I ran my fingers through the fur.

"I'm getting jealous of the rug, sweetheart."

"How do you and Pepper know each other?" I blew out a breath.

"It's not what you think." He sat beside me on the bed.

His bed. With him in touching distance. Kissing distance. So close as he was wont to be, but never touching me unless he eased the pain of my past by holding my wrists with great care. I wanted to take his pain away, and yet I'd still asked about the witch.

"You flirt with her, you let her touch you. You appear to have known each other for some time. Was she your former lover?"

"And if I said she was?" He quirked an eyebrow.

My hands glowed with my power.

Sledge chuckled. "You're hot when you're jealous, but you have nothing to be jealous of with Pepper. She's more like an annoying cousin to me."

I shoved my hands under my legs. "Are you related?"

"Way back in the ancient times her grandmere's grandmere's sister mated with my something or other on ma's side. I don't pay attention to that crap. So, yeah, Pepper and I are distantly related and makes us off-limits, which was never an issue anyway, in case you were wondering."

"Thank you for telling me." I leaned over and kissed his cheek.

He froze.

I touched my lips to his cheek again. Rightness zinged through my entire body. I nibbled my way to the edge of his lips.

"Bree." Sledge gripped the covers. "What are you doing, sweetheart? You can't do this now. I'm operating on a razor's edge when it comes to you as it is and after tonight I'm about to slice myself open."

Cupping his jaw with both hands, I said, "I want to do the right thing for you."

"We shouldn't. I put Ma and Dad in a room after cleaning the blood off his body. Heidi's here too."

"You want me to leave?" I let go of his face.

"No. I want you to tell me you're mine and beg me to touch you. Ask me to rip off your dress and devour you. I long to bite you so hard and so many times you'll always remember our first time."

My body hummed in approval and my power did too, making my hands glow.

"But ... but if you say those words to me, you can't mark me as yours until after my dad wakes. With him out of action, I'm next in line to be Alpha. I can't go to the Quiet as Arrow did right now."

I smoothed my hand through the rug. The soft fur comforted me.

"I understand," I said as I stood.

Sledge let out a noise that said he realized I'd never say what he wanted to hear. He was wrong. I was wrong to deny this so long. I urged his knees apart and stepped closer. He gazed up at me with such passion, my legs quivered.

"I'm your mate and you are mine." The words rang with so much truth they hurt my ears.

Sledge smiled. "Before you say the rest, and I'm rock hard for you already waiting for those words, I have to warn you I don't think I can give you gentle at the moment."

I slid my dress from my shoulders letting the material pool at my waist. "I won't break, I'm a Fae and immortal. Now touch me, Sledge."

He let out the longest breath and lifted his hands to hover over my breast. My nipples ached from the heat radiating from his palms. His palms were massive, he could cup my breasts with ease, but his hands hovered. Teasing and igniting the thrum of desire clenching my body and pounding deep inside my channel until moisture seeped between my legs.

"Please, Sledge. Please, touch me."

CHAPTER FIFTEEN

SLEDGE

THE WORDS I'D WANTED to hear from her the moment I'd made my stupid promise. I longed to hear her say them again and again until she embedded them in my brain. My mate asking me to touch her. To pleasure her. To drop her to her knees as she'd done to me. A claw burst from my index finger, and I slashed the front of her dress. The gauzy material fell to the floor in a cloud of green. Green so like her power over nature.

I ran my nail from the top of her collarbone down the center of her body, through the milky valley of her breasts, over the tightness of her stomach muscles, the small indent of her belly button, to the top of her silvery-blonde curls. Her skin pebbled in the wake of my touch. So sensitive and responsive to her mate. My cock ached with a ferocious need for her and her alone.

"I'm so hard for you, sweetheart."

"Let me care for you." She dropped to her knees.

My wolf chuffed in satisfaction with her submissive pose. She tugged my shorts down and wrapped her mouth around me without preamble. No tentative lick of her tongue, no soft kiss of her lips. She was all warmth and moisture around my cock, swallowing me up. I threaded my fingers in her hair and urged her faster, harder. She pressed her hands into my hips so hard there'd be imprints from her nails. I loved it. I shoved up into her mouth with a roar of release.

Having my mate give in to me had me still hard. I shoved her back onto the floor and kissed her mouth. She met me stroke for stroke. My essence still coated her tongue. She thrust it into my mouth until we both panted for air.

I broke our kiss to latch onto her hard nipple. Her back bowed and her fingers dug into the side of my head. My mate could give as good as I was going to give her. She was perfect. I sunk my teeth into the mound of her flesh. She let out a high-pitched scream of pleasure and stroked her legs to my hips urging me closer until my hard cock rubbed along her slick entrance. I longed to mark her in so many ways she'd never question she was mine.

Releasing my teeth, I lapped at her breast. Circled the hard peak with my tongue until her hips rolled harder under mine. I grabbed her legs and forced them to her ears, sitting back to take in the sight of my mate spread open, willing and ready for me to fill.

"Do you realize how many times I've scented your arousal?"

She dropped her head to the floor. "That's cheating, wolf shifter."

"I can't help using my wolf shifter talents." I smirked.

She peered down the length of her body to my face and raised her eyebrows. "What talents?"

"Sweet thing, you've asked for it now."

I shoved my face into her damp heat and inhaled the spicy allure of her arousal. One swipe of my tongue and she whimpered. Her taste was heady. I didn't lick her with finesse. I licked her like a man gone insane. And I was. Insane for my mate. Her legs shook in my hands. She was close to coming, but it was too soon. I stopped licking her slickness and bit the soft skin on the inside of her thigh. She smacked the floor with her glowing palms.

"Damn, sneaky wolf." Her chest heaved.

"You've made me wait a long time for this. You can wait."

I let go of her legs and stood. Having her on the floor beneath my feet, slick and ready for me made my wolf rumble in satisfaction. Briana's eyes widened, but she didn't scramble away from my beast. If anything, her scent grew more robust. I bent and scooped her up off the floor. Her naked body slid against mine, rubbing and teasing me to take what my mate offered.

And take I would. I backed her up to the wall, her back hitting it with a thud. She wrapped her legs around my waist lining herself up with my hard cock. I spread her ass cheeks, opening her further and thrust into her so hard, I hit the end of her cervix. My body surged.

I couldn't wait to fill her up with my release. First, I wanted to rock her world.

I pounded into her hard. The painting on the wall wobbled from the hook and bounced to the floor. Briana scratched my back with her nails in a long deep score from neck to ass. Then she dug her nails into my ass and urged me faster.

Perfect. So perfect.

I changed the angle of my hips to rub against her clit. She moaned aloud. Her enthusiastic cry gusted against my ear. Then she clamped her teeth on my lobe. My mate wanted to play. Well, play I would. Her body was slick with sweat. Her moans and pants grew louder. Hotter. Her body trembled.

So I stopped.

She slapped my chest with her glowing palms.

"Don't mark me, sweetheart." I released her legs and stepped back. Her slick moisture glistened on my hard cock. Fuck, if that didn't make me harder still. "But I'm marking you."

I spun her around and marched her to the bed. Shoved her head to the mattress and jerked her hips to my cock. She took my cock like a good mate. Her sheath clenching and releasing with each slide in and out. I covered her with the weight of my body along her back. She shivered. I smoothed my lips to the back of her neck. Ran my teeth on the sensitive curve where her shoulder met her neck.

"I'm going to bite you here," I said sliding my hands between her and the mattress. One hand found a hard nipple while the other found her hard clit. "Ask me to bite you. Ask me to mark you as mine." I pinched her nipple between my finger and thumb.

"Sledge," she gasped.

"I need the words." I stroked her slick clit.

Her hips bucked backward shoving me in deeper.

"Bite me, please."

I squeezed her nipple tighter. "And?"

She moaned. "Mark me as yours."

I sunk my teeth into her neck, breaking the skin with the force of my bite. I wasn't meant to bite her so hard, but this mark would be ragged and raw like the way we fucked. Savoring the feel of my teeth and cock in her at the same time, I pounded my cock into her. Briana whimpered under my bite. Her body tensed and shook with the pleasure my bite produced for her. I felt her pleasure as much as I felt mine. I now joined us in the way of wolf shifters.

My cock surged harder, more insistent I let go inside my mate.

And she was truly mine now.

Mine for the rest of time.

I growled around her skin in my mouth.

"Harder," Briana begged.

I sunk my teeth in harder. Pounded her harder. I tightened my grip on her nipple until she lost herself to the peak of pleasure and pain mingled together. Then and only then did I pinch her clit, sending her into the realm of pleasure so intense she lost control of her body in a shaking, quivering contraction of muscles from inside and out, and a scream that was a long time coming. I raised my head and howled my release, letting her orgasm take mine from my body with enough force my legs shook, and I struggled to hold my weight. I sagged against her back, pressing her into the mattress with way too much mass than I should for Briana's slender frame. A deep sigh left her mouth as though she wanted me there.

In due course, I dragged my hands out from under her body making her jerk with sensitivity. I forced myself off her back, took a moment to enjoy the sight of my mark on the back of her neck before I withdrew from her body. She rolled over with a sated smile on her face.

"Are you all right, sweetheart?"

Her smile grew. "I've never been more all right. How is that possible?"

"Because you're with your mate." I settled on the bed and dragged her into my arms.

She rested her head on my chest. "I'm sorry it took me this long."

I ran a hand down her back. "Don't sweat it, sweet thing." I pinched her bottom.

She yelped.

"I intend to make you pay in the most pleasurable ways."

"Sledge?" She rolled onto my chest and stared into my eyes. "What happened out there tonight?"

I shoved my hands behind my head and enjoyed the sight of her naked and sprawled across me.

"I don't know. Heidi and I were racing through the trees. The little punk thought she could outrun me. We'd already taken down a wild pig. The pack was headed back to town with the kill. I thought Dad was with the pack, but he must have been behind us, keeping an eye on Heidi. I would have kept her safe. If it wasn't for my hearing, I would never have caught the weird crunch of branches. I made Heidi turn back with me and we found Dad at the bottom of a small drop off a rock face."

She brushed a hand over my face.

"I understand nature." She bit her lip. "That branch was no act of nature."

"What do you mean?"

"You probably didn't take the time to look, but the limb had been cut."

I frowned. "You think someone injured him on purpose?"

"I do. There is no way the branch would have formed that way in nature."

"You disintegrated the limb so we have no evidence."

"'Twas the only way to remove it without harm."

"Thank you." I cupped her face and brought her lips to mine, kissing her with a gentleness I wasn't capable of earlier.

She bit my lip.

I rolled her over. "You want to play rough again?"

"What about your father?"

"We'll head out to the forest tomorrow and check out the scene. With any luck, there are clues out there, and I'll talk to everyone in the pack."

"You already suspect someone in your pack?" she asked, too smart to miss anything.

"Yes," I said with a scowl. Eloise was my prime suspect.

"I'll help in any way I can."

And she would. My mate. She'd allowed our connection to form even before today. Briana might not realize it, but I was utterly in love with her. Her strength, her passion, her family loyalty. She was fated for me. As all mates were. But we formed love, it wasn't a given from the get-go.

"Ready for round two?"

She nipped the side of my neck. "I've been ready since round one."

I laughed and cupped the back of her neck. Even with my father lying unconscious from a probable attempt on his life, and the weight of the pack hanging around my neck, she made me laugh. Such a small thing, but such a big thing for the future of our mateship.

A future we'd form together.

But first, I needed to teach my mate another lesson in teasing a wolf shifter. By the end of the night, I'd cover her in bite marks. My bite marks. My wolf chuffed with satisfaction.

You and me both, buddy.

CHAPTER SIXTEEN
BRIANA

W HILE SLEDGE WAS A demanding and controlling lover, he was also attentive to every movement of my body, every need pulsing through my skin and rippling from my inside out. His bites, while painful, were also pleasing. How I longed to feel his teeth buried in my skin again, and again.

Except he wasn't in the bedroom when I woke.

I slipped on a gray t-shirt from his closet since my dress lay in shreds from his claws and padded out of his room. Voices echoed from the kitchen. I hesitated, then proceeded to the kitchen. I needed to see my mate. The influence of the mark on my neck let me comprehend I was indeed his now. My power hummed in approval. A constant zing put a bounce in my step. Or perhaps it was the night of hard loving putting a bounce in my step.

I'd never experienced a lover like Sledge.

I wanted only him now.

Why had I fought him so hard?

"Good morning, sweetheart." Sledge grinned from where he sat at the table with a stack of pancakes on his plate.

"Good morning." I brushed my hair back and tucked it behind my ears.

His mom dropped the spatula at the stove and raced across the kitchen to encircle me in her arms. "Welcome to the family."

"Ah, thank you." I shifted in her tight embrace. *How strong were all these wolf shifters?*

She let go of the maternal hug and rushed back to flip the pancake. "I hoped that's what happened last night."

My cheeks heated.

She shook the spatula. "The wolves on the other side of town would have heard you two."

Sledge laughed. I sunk onto the chair beside him. I'd never screamed in the throes of passion until Sledge, and he'd made me scream many times last night. He draped an arm around my shoulders and kissed the top of my head.

"No need to be embarrassed." He grinned.

"I may bury myself under a mound of flowers."

"I'd still find you." Sledge nuzzled my hair.

"I'm sure you would with your sneaky wolf nose." I plucked a piece of pancake from his plate.

"Hey, stealing my food now?"

"Aye. You're mine now, so is your food."

Kelly chuckled and placed the fresh pancake on Sledge's pile. Sledge dove for it and she slapped his hand with the spatula.

"Offer it to your mate first." She tutted.

"Ma," Sledge whined. "I'm a growing boy. I need all the pancakes."

"You've done all the growing you can."

I snagged the pancake and smirked.

Kelly smiled and walked back to the stove.

Sledge ran his tongue up my neck, and whispered, "You'll pay later."

I raised my eyebrow and whispered, "I'm looking forward to it."

Heidi wandered into the kitchen dressed in a sunshine yellow skirt and blouse. Her entire demeanor was sad despite the bright color of her outfit. I glanced down at my hastily donned t-shirt to Sledge's jeans and shirt. Kelly was dressed in jeans and a blouse.

"Did you bring clothes here?" I asked.

"No. We keep clothes here. Wolf shifters need to keep clothes in various locations," Kelly said.

Heidi slumped onto the chair opposite me.

"Hey, little princess. How are you?" I asked.

Heidi lifted her sad eyes, jumped out of the chair and hugged me. "Thanks for saving my dad," she blubbered through tears. "I'm sorry I said I hated you. I don't hate you. You're amazing. Your power is amazing. And my brother likes you. I like you too."

I patted her back. "Shh, it's okay. It wasn't your fault what happened to your father."

Sledge gripped my thigh. I didn't need the warning to not mention anything untoward.

Her sobs quietened as I smoothed my hand down her hair over and over.

"I know you didn't really mean it."

She sniffed and nodded against my shoulder then straightened and returned to her chair.

"Accidents happen." Kelly stepped behind her daughter, wrapped her arms around Heidi's shoulders and rested her chin on top of her head. "Your father will be okay."

Heidi's bottom lip wobbled again as more tears threatened to spill.

Sledge stood and fetched the koala from the crate and shoved it into Heidi's arms. "Say goodbye to this guy. I'm releasing him today."

"You are?" Heidi perked up. "He's all healed."

"Yep, just like Dad will be." Sledge ruffled her hair. "Briana and I are heading out after breakfast to let him go."

"Sledge, you'll have to address the pack," Kelly said releasing her daughter and folding her arms over her chest. "They need to know what happened."

"I will when I get back. Are you guys staying here or heading home?"

Heidi screwed up her face. "Can we go home, Ma? Headphones didn't even drown out those two."

Kelly smiled. "Sure. Ray is stable enough to move."

"I'll get the doc to give him a once over then get the pack to transfer him. I'll make some calls and get everything organized." Sledge stood. "Let's get a wriggle on, Bree. I have a lot to do today."

"Let me put on a dress and I'll be ready."

A quick wardrobe change later and Sledge and I were rumbling along in his truck with the koala in the backseat.

"I didn't realize my sister said she hated you." He squeezed my hand then gripped the steering wheel again. "I'm sorry."

"It's not your fault. Besides, I wasn't the nicest to her when we first met wrapping her up in a tree."

Sledge laughed. "You did the same to me."

"I remember." My body warmed at the way I'd tied him to the tree. I cleared my throat. "I'll miss seeing the little guy at the house."

Sledge smirked like he knew where my thoughts had wandered. "Don't worry, there will be more koalas sooner or later to care for."

"That's sad."

"Yeah, wildfires are the most harmful to them out here in Crystal Creek." Sledge turned onto a dirt track out near Arrow's house and drove deeper into the forest.

The track narrowed until the truck wouldn't fit through the thick bush. Sledge stopped the truck, climbed out, swung open my door and offered me his hand. I climbed out. He hauled me against his body and his lips met mine. We kissed like we needed each other to breathe. I hummed in pleasure recalling the mind-shattering orgasms he'd toyed from my body. Sledge broke the kiss and fetched the koala's cage from the back seat and headed into the forest.

"Sledge," I hissed and caught up with him.

"Yes, sweet thing?" He whistled and kept walking.

I flung my power into the branches of the next tree and tripped him over. He stumbled, juggled the cage, and landed on his back with the cage held over his head. I took advantage and unzipped his pants.

"Bree, we have a koala to release."

"You release him. I'm releasing something else."

He growled and lowered the cage on the ground. I tugged at his jeans. Sledge laughed. He wouldn't be laughing soon. I called my power to slither vines across the ground and wrapped them around his wrists and ankles. He tugged on his binds.

"You want to be in control this time?" he asked.

"Aye." I unbuttoned his shirt and ran my hands over his muscles.

"Have at it, princess."

"I will." I brushed my lips to his chest and ran my tongue around his nipple.

"You'd prefer me to tease your nipples," he said lowering his voice.

I proceeded to the other nipple. He was right. I scraped my teeth down his six-pack stomach. His muscles twitched. His hard cock throbbed. I ran my nails up and down his hard length until pre-cum glistened on his tip. With a smirk, I lowered my head and licked his thick crown.

He tugged his wrists on the vines until they creaked, but they held. For now. They'd give sooner or later with his strength, but for now, it was my turn to tease my mate. I lowered my tongue to his balls and lapped them like they were the biggest, juiciest blueberries I'd ever tasted until my saliva dripped between the hard globes of his ass. I slid a hand to the wetness and coaxed his asshole to take my finger, crooked it inside, and rub it against his prostate.

"You play dirty." He panted.

I covered his throbbing cock with my mouth and held him there all the while stroking the pleasure spot inside him until he jerked so hard with a release the vines snapped and his hands landed on the sides of my face holding me still to the raging release of his orgasm. I swirled my tongue around his tip. He yanked my head off his sensitive organ and sat up, dislodging my finger, and rolled me onto the ground, his chest heaving with the force of his orgasm.

"My mate knows tricks."

I licked the last of his essence from my lips. "I've been around a long time."

Sledge snorted. "Understatement." He ran his hands up my legs, dragging my dress to my waist. "What other tricks do you have up this pretty dress of yours?"

"All sorts." I lifted my legs around his waist and rubbed against his thickening cock.

"Yeah?" He wriggled a hand between us and sunk two fingers into my welcoming wetness. "I'm going to fuck you with my fingers until you're asking for my cock."

Moisture flooded and slicked his fingers further.

"You like it when I talk dirty to you?"

"Aye." I pressed against his fingers wanting him to go harder and faster.

"You're the hottest thing I've ever felt." He curled his fingers and massaged his thumb to my clit. "The way your body tightens around mine, and the way your scent grows heavy with arousal. Hottest thing I've ever tasted too. All that sweet desire for me."

My breathing grew ragged, and the roll of my hips lost themselves to the pleasure building. "Sledge," I said, begging. "I want your cock."

He hauled me off the ground, tugged my dress over my head, kicked my legs out from under me while holding my waist, and lowered me to a fallen log, bending me over it. My knees, stomach, and chest scraped against the rough bark. Sledge's finger thrust into my wetness again.

"Sledge, your cock."

"Where, Bree? Here?" He dragged his finger up to my ass. "Or here?"

"Anywhere. I need you inside me now."

He shoved into me with a roughness that was all Sledge. My toes curled at the rigorous breach. He thrust hard and fast giving me no time to adjust to his thick cock. His finger rubbed in time to his cock pounding a rhythm to the frantic beats of my heart.

"Just remember," Sledge panted. "You started this."

My muscles tightened. The pleasure zinged through my veins. My clit throbbed against his thumb. My vision faded to black. There was only Sledge. Only my mate taking me in any way he wanted.

And I wanted them all.

I wanted his lips, his tongue, his teeth, and his hard cock on every place of my body.

"You're close to coming, aren't you?"

"Aye."

"I should stop." He grunted and kept thrusting. "But I can't."

He brushed my hair from the back of my neck and bit the soft spot under my ear. My body shook. Spiraled hotter. Tighter. I couldn't breathe. Oxygen no longer mattered. All that mattered was this pleasure. The peak of insanity as Sledge worked my body into release. My mind blanked. The pleasure too much, I cried out. Tears trickled from my eyes. Lack of oxygen and my cries parched my throat. My orgasm spasmed on his fingers and around his cock buried in me as every muscle in my body contracted and released over and over again, making my toes curl.

Sledge howled his release to the forest and filled me with his hotness, scorching a trail in my sensitive flesh. He draped his body over mine, a blanket of muscle and man, and kissed the side of my face until I turned my head and met his lips.

"I'm crushing you." He rolled over and hauled me into his lap. "You're scratched by the bark." He stroked a hand down my front. "Are you hurt? Am I too rough?"

"No, Sledge." I cupped his cheek. "I could have smoothed the bark with my power if I needed."

"Right." He chuckled. "I keep forgetting your power."

I stroked my hand down his chest. He grabbed my hand and kissed my knuckles.

"As much as I'd like to keep fucking you into submission. We have a koala to release. A potential attempted murder to investigate. And we could both do with a rinse in the lake."

"Aye." Scratches marred my skin with smudges of dirt, and pieces of bark and leaves littered my hair. "A dip sounds good. You'll have to let go so we can stand up."

"I'm never letting go." He jerked to his feet with me in his arms.

I laughed. "You can't carry me around naked all day."

"Watch me." He strode down the dirt path.

"Sledge." I slapped his chest. "The koala."

"Right." He stopped and turned back to the crate. "Sorry little guy. I should have let you go before making you watch our porn show."

I laughed harder. Sledge lowered me to my feet, and I shimmied into my dress. He shot me an unhappy look but yanked on his jeans. Dia, he was a specimen in and out of clothes.

He picked up the crate and winked at me. "Stop checking out my sexy ass."

I rolled my eyes. "Your ego knows no boundaries."

"Hey, I recall a certain mate enjoying my ass not that long ago."

I puffed out a laugh. "As I recall, you enjoyed it more."

"I've never come so hard in my life. You're full of surprises. Our life together will be amazing." He walked along the path.

I followed behind him. Our life together. Which meant here, on Earth. An ache for the Summer Court tugged in my chest. By agreeing to be Sledge's mate, I'd made myself an outcast like Saoirse. *How would I cope without seeing my mother and father, my brothers and sisters?* They'd been my constant support since my loss. My breathing became shallower, and I rubbed my wrists.

Sledge spun around. "Why the freak out?" He scanned the trees. "There's no fire."

"It's not that." I rubbed the skin. "It's this. Us. I'll be stuck here like Saoirse."

Sledge put the crate on the ground, opened the door, and let the koala out to climb the nearest tree. He turned his full attention to me and held out his hands. I laid my wrists in his palms such a familiar habit now I didn't even think of denying my need to have him soothe me.

"Breathe. You're not stuck here. No one knows I'm your mate back home, right? So, you can pretend when you go home."

"You'll let me go home?"

"Sweetheart, I'm not a dictator. You can come and go as you please and know I'll be waiting here for you."

"You're such a sweet man." I met his gaze.

"Wolf shifter." He curled his lip to show his pointed teeth.

A shiver of need flickered through my body. His thumbs closed around my wrist and stroked the frantic rush of my pulse.

"Is this okay?" he asked.

I glanced down at his hands wrapped around my wrists. It occurred to me then, he'd never circled my wrists before. Only held them in the comfort and warmth of his palm. I should be freaking out. I should remember the time the Trappers restrained me, but I wasn't. Sledge's presence soothed every place he touched.

"Aye," I whispered.

"Good. Let's go for a dip."

We followed the track to the sandy soil surrounding the lake. Sledge stripped, and I watched him stride into the water naked before joining him. The water was icy, the spring sunshine barely heated the surface. Lucky for me, I didn't feel the cold. Sledge drew me into his arms, and we bobbed in the water until his skin cooled beneath my hands on his shoulders.

"We should go," I said with regret. Holding Sledge and being held by him was almost as good as the sex.

"Yeah." He brushed a sweet kiss to my cheek. "I've put it off long enough."

We sloshed through the water and picked up our clothes.

"I forgot the towels." Sledge sighed. "They're in the truck."

"We'll walk back and dry off."

He groaned. "You want to walk around naked and not expect me to throw you to the ground again."

My body warmed, and I almost asked him to do that here on the waterfront of the lake. Instead, I slipped on my dress and set off down the path. Sledge caught up to me carrying his clothes.

"You'll catch a chill."

I laughed. "No such thing for a Fae."

"Right."

I watched the beads of water drip from his body onto the ground with each step he took. If we didn't hurry, I'd be the one throwing him to the forest floor again.

Sledge inhaled. "Sweet thing, stop thinking dirty thoughts about your mate. Until later, that is."

"I'll never be able to hide anything from you, will I?"

"Why would you?"

We arrived at the truck, and he fetched a towel from the back and scrubbed himself dry.

"'Tis a little unfair with your wolf senses, and when I mark you, you'll know everything about me, but I'll never have that connection with you."

He wrapped a towel around the long length of my hair and patted it dry. "You already have a connection." He brushed his thumb over the bite mark on my neck. "Anything you want to know I'll tell you."

A flare of power so strong from the bite mark on my neck sent a quiver to my body. He was right, the connection in his bite mark was more than a scar and a warning to other males I belonged to him. Deep inside there was a connection to Sledge through my mind and heart. The way it beat was for him and him alone now.

"Let's head to the location of your father's accident."

"Shit," he said throwing the damp towels in the truck and dressing. "What if you're right?"

He headed in the other direction from the lake.

"Then you'll need to protect your father."

"I already told a select few to stand guard at his house discreetly. Hopefully, Ma doesn't catch sight of them."

"Wise move."

He held a branch back for me to duck through the forest. I could use my power to clear our path, but as I didn't know the location of the accident, I didn't want to risk disturbing the scene and any evidence. The scent of eucalyptus grew heavier as he crushed a few leaves in his hand.

"It's just up ahead another few steps and down there." He pointed to a rocky outcrop.

"Stay here and let me look at the vegetation first."

"Fine." He folded his arms and leaned against the thick trunk of a tree.

Footprints and paw prints littered the soft soil. I followed the trail and studied every tree and bush in the dense scrub. A few branches were snapped at the height Sledge would have carried his father through the forest. That was understandable. I inched closer. There in the soil was a dainty female footprint. I bent and studied it. It could be Kelly's. It was too big for Heidi's feet.

"Do you know what your ma's footprint looks like?" I called out.

"Like a woman's," he called back.

I rolled my eyes. No help. I ventured further. The woman's footprint disappeared over the edge. I climbed down the small incline. At the bottom, there was a dark patch in the soil. The Alpha's blood. Heavy male footprints were indented next to the patch. Sledge's footprints and to the side of his, half-buried under his footprint was the smaller female one.

"Did your ma come down here?"

"No," he called out.

I sighed. It seemed more and more probable a woman might be the culprit. Besides the footprint, there was no further evidence of foul play. The branches down here weren't even the same as the one Ray had embedded in his chest. I wished I hadn't disintegrated the damn thing now.

"There's nothing down here apart from the same female footprint as above. Which could be your ma's."

Sledge's head appeared above me, and he held a hand out to me. I placed my hand in his and let him haul me up.

"Do you still think it was deliberate?" he asked.

"Aye. The branch in his chest wasn't from any of these trees nearby. If he fell and landed on the branch, then it would be from a nearby tree. I can't prove it though. Plus." I pointed at the short distance. "Do you believe a strong Alpha wolf would suffer such a grievous injury from such a brief fall?"

He frowned. "I didn't take the time to consider it last night. It was dark, Dad was hurt. But, yeah, you're right."

"My guess, and it's speculation from the footprints, is a woman ambushed your Alpha, pushed him over the ledge, jumped down, and stabbed him with the branch." I pursed my lips because it sounded ridiculous even to me.

CHAPTER SEVENTEEN
SLEDGE

I DROPPED BRIANA AT Arrow's house and left to deal with the pack business. My wolf was happy to be running things, even if it was for a little while. His alpha tendencies made him puff his chest out in pride. Dad had given me all the tools I needed to keep the pack in line. Even if I'd listened to my wolf and done my own thing, I had learned from him.

What he wasn't happy about was leaving his mate. Even for a little while. I wasn't happy either, but she needed to be with her sister, and I respected her commitment to her family. One day, we'd have a family of our own. I couldn't wait to see her looking like a round blueberry carrying our child. But I was getting ahead of myself. She'd finally accepted our mating, and I wouldn't push her for more knowing she'd already lost a child. She might be more fearful than Saoirse in getting pregnant.

Besides, she wasn't in heat, and she'd said she didn't have heats anymore. Her words were lies. But why did she lie about that?

A problem I needed to shelve for now. My focus needed to be on the pack and if there was a threat to Dad.

I sat in Dad's office chair. It was strange being on this side of the desk. Jessa was way too eager to please me in the office, telling me the next pack member was here for me to question about last night.

"Jessa, sit down. We need to talk."

"Sure thing, Sledge." She perched on the chair, her short dress hiking up her thigh as she crossed her legs.

I avoided looking at the expanse of skin. Not that I wanted to. There was no simple way to let a woman down.

"I mated," I said.

She stood with a start. "To whom? Not Eloise?"

"No. To Briana."

"Oh." Her lips trembled.

"I thought I should tell you since we were close in high school."

"Yeah, sure." She wrapped her arms around her waist. "I'll, ah, send the next one in. I mean Jonathon."

She flung open the door so fast, her long brown hair fluttered in the breeze she'd created.

Jonathon walked into the office.

"Take a seat. This is just a formality considering the events of last night. All I need is for you to tell me how you remember last night."

Jonathon sat and told me how he and Clara enjoyed the hunt. I sighed. Not one pack member experienced anything bad about the hunt. It'd been a good night. A successful hunt. The wolves were happy. News of the Alpha's accident didn't get through to them until this morning. Jonathon jiggled his right knee and tapped his left leg. The young recruit was nervous about something. I didn't need my wolf nose to scent that.

"Anything else you'd like to add?"

"I, ah, overheard Eloise talking to Clara this morning when I woke up."

"What did you hear?" I sat up straighter.

His knee jiggled faster. "You can't tell Clara I told you. I feel like I'm betraying my mate."

"I get it," I said, softening my voice. "I won't say a thing."

"Clara asked Eloise why she wasn't on the hunt."

"She wasn't?" I sat forward.

"I don't remember seeing her wolf."

Now that he said that, I didn't remember seeing her wolf either. She'd been at the party in the town square though. I remember her flirting with me, chatting with me about the party and how happy she was to be here. Most importantly I recalled Briana getting jealous. She had nothing to worry about. It was why I'd left Eloise and ventured over to Briana because I'd sensed her unease.

"What was her answer?"

"She said she had a meeting with someone. She wouldn't tell Clara who, even when she kept asking.

Clara wanted to know if she'd found her mate. I think Clara's had enough of waiting. I sure have."

Another thing I understood. The urge to mark your mate. It was hard not doing it the moment you realized they were yours.

"Don't wait then. Eloise will be fine. I'll make sure of it." If she had anything to do with my dad's accident, then I'd make sure she was fine behind the bars of our jail. Where she'd stay for the rest of her life. She'd be fine indeed locked away.

"Do you know who she's meeting?"

"Me? No."

I sat back in my chair and gazed out the window. Every inch of my body was tense. I'd been here long enough asking questions and getting no answers to help. I needed to act. My wolf was restless. Eager to hunt the person responsible for my dad's injuries. It was going to be hard to stop him from ripping out that person's throat when I found them.

"Can you do me a favor?" I swung my gaze back to Jonathon.

"Sure."

"Can you get Clara and Eloise to the Pup's Tavern tonight?"

His eyebrows rose. "Shouldn't be a problem. They like going there."

"Good. I'll see you later tonight." I nodded.

Jonathon rose and made his way to the door.

"And Jonathon, don't mention me asking you to take them there."

"Okay."

Jonathon left the office. My office for now. How things had changed in a day. Me running the Crystal Creek wolf pack, and mated to an amazing woman with powers I loved to feel up against my body. I couldn't wait for Briana to mark me as hers. If it wasn't for this dilemma, I'd have insisted she'd do it straight away. Not that I thought she'd change her mind now. No, she was mine as I was hers.

I didn't relish what I'd have to do tonight. Briana would understand my need to protect my family, but I still didn't like it. I left the office and drove to Arrow's house.

"Hey, how's Saoirse?" I asked walking into their house.

"She's okay. Worried. But okay." Arrow led me to the kitchen. "Drink?"

"Sure."

"I figured you could use one after last night." He grabbed two beer bottles from the refrigerator. "Briana filled us in."

"Yeah, it was a shitty night. Dad's stable, but who knows when he'll wake. Which leaves me in charge of the pack." I took the beer.

"I'll have your back."

"As I'll always have yours. I need back up tonight at the tavern."

"Done," he said without hesitation or questions.

We clinked our beer bottles.

"So you marked Briana." He smirked.

"Yeah. Did she tell you that too?"

"No need, dude. Her sexed-up smile was enough of a giveaway and the jagged bite mark on her neck. Saoirse got excited. She's happy to have a family member live here with her."

I drained half the beer. "She might not stay here all the time."

"Why not?"

"She has family and responsibilities in her home."

"Your wolf will go psycho when she leaves." He tugged on the beer label.

"I'll handle him."

"Shit, Sledge, leaving Saoirse to go to work is hard enough, let alone the times she disappeared to the Summer Court." He shook his head. "What if she doesn't come back? What if her father puts her in jail like he did Saoirse?"

I gulped the beer and slammed it on the benchtop. "No one will realize she's mated. She's not telling any of them. And I need to trust she'll come back."

"You've really got a handle on all this," he stated.

I nodded even though I didn't need to, but Arrow was my best mate, he'd seen how wild I was in my younger years. Up until recently really. Funny what finding a mate can do to a wolf shifter.

"Can she stay here with you tonight? I need to do some pack business."

"Yeah. What pack business?"

"Something that might upset Briana."

Briana strode into the kitchen. "What will upset me?"

"Shit." I stepped around Arrow to face Briana. "I can't say."

She narrowed her eyes. "If I asked, you'd tell me?"

"Yeah, I said I would tell you anything if you asked."

"But you don't want to tell me."

"No."

Her gaze searched my face from the pull of my brow to the tightness of my mouth. She cupped her hand to my cheek. I nudged into the comfort of her palm.

"I won't ask."

"Thank you, princess. Stay here tonight and spend time with your sister."

She frowned.

I kissed her cheek and strode for the front door.

"Sledge," she said. "Be careful."

"I will, sweetheart." I slipped out the front door before I second-guessed my plan.

Half the pack filled the tavern. Angus was having a hard time behind the bar keeping up with all the orders. On nights like this, he could do with a hand, but that was his decision to employ help, and I understood how intent he was on keeping his bar to himself. Silly old codger. As if any of us would take it from him.

I sat at the bar and made small talk with anyone who ventured my way. Most said a friendly hello, asked how my dad was, ordered their drink, and moved on. I got it. They were all unsettled with Ray unconscious. Hell, I had a hard enough time, but I needed to keep my shit together. Briana was waiting for me at Arrow's house. My cock twitched in my pants. Now, so wasn't the time to let my thoughts wander to my mate and her slick body.

Jonathon walked into the bar, his arm around Clara's waist, with Eloise trailing behind. I caught her gaze and smiled in welcome. She fluttered a smile and made a beeline for me. Like luring a fish with bait.

"Hey, Sledge" She slid onto the stool next to me and placed her hand on my arm. "How are you holding up?"

"Eh." I shrugged and signaled Angus over. "Can I get you a drink?"

She beamed. "Yes, please."

I held up two fingers and Angus slid two beer bottles onto the wooden bar with a grunt. Guess he was a part of the don't like Eloise club. I handed her a bottle, stroking her fingers on purpose. I stifled the shudder of revulsion running into my stomach.

For the next two hours, I flirted with Eloise in a way I'd never done before. Eloise lapped it up. Angus shot me a filthy look every time he placed more beers on the bar. He didn't understand what I was up to, and I couldn't explain like I couldn't explain to Briana. I didn't want her to know. *What if she walked in and saw me flirting with another woman? What if she hated me for this?* I couldn't keep up this charade for the rest of the night or any other night for that matter, but I needed to protect my family. Mom and Dad counted on me. So did Heidi.

I wouldn't let them down.

I leaned in close to Eloise. "Want to head back to my place?"

"Sledge." She fluttered her lashes. "What type of girl do you take me for?"

Shit. I didn't expect her to put the brakes on now.

I held up my hands. "At least let me walk you home."

"That's more like it." She stood. "You need to treat your future mate with respect."

I swallowed the rise of bile, shoved back my stool, and escorted her out of the bar. The forest was dark, the moon hidden behind a thick blanket of clouds. We followed the dirt road back into town. Angus was adamant to keep his tavern away from town. He was old enough that when the town grew, he told them to build it away from him. If he didn't love serving booze so much, he'd be a hermit. He liked that he could send everyone home at the end of the night and not have us come back until the next night.

Eloise tripped. I grabbed her arm to hold her upright. She slid her arm around my waist. Stupid falling for her move. She could have stabbed me in the side if she was Dad's would-be assassin. The petite woman didn't seem capable of overpowering an alpha wolf.

Still ...

I wouldn't put it past her.

Shadows flitted through the trees. My backup was here. Arrow would have been too noticeable if there was moonlight. I'd picked the perfect night.

"I missed seeing your pretty wolf in the hunt last night. She sure is a beauty."

Eloise giggled. "You're such a charmer."

"What? I can't help it around pretty wolf shifters like you."

"I thought you might be interested in the Fae." Her arm tightened around my waist.

"I was keeping an eye on her for the Alpha. I'm all about the wolf." To prove my point, I curled my lips and howled.

Eloise let out a resounding yip.

If my wolf was interested in her, that particular yip would have set his hormones racing.

"I'll need a pretty wolf like you as a mate now I'm Alpha." My lies had to be catching her ears, but she fluttered her eyelashes at me.

"You do." She squeezed my butt.

Bile rose in my throat.

"I've wanted to be Alpha a long time."

"Oh, Sledge," she said, stepping into me. "Mark me now then we can rule the pack together." She brushed her hair from her neck.

Shit, how did I keep up the pretense? How would I get her to spill her secrets? I'd have to play along for now. For the safety of my dad because seeing him almost dead changed me, made me realize how easy something could rip life away from us in an instant even when we were immortal. I'd do almost anything to keep the ones I loved safe.

I lowered my lips to her neck. Vomit gathered in my stomach. She shivered in my arms, under my mouth. This was so wrong. I couldn't mark her. But I'd pretend until she spilled her secrets. I ran my teeth along her neck. So long as she let me lead then there was no chance I'd accidentally bite her.

"Like this?"

"Yes," she whimpered.

"I'll need a mate to help me."

"I already did." She sighed.

I forced my teeth against her skin as I battled against the rage to rip her throat out just for trying to take me away from Briana, then murmured, "How did you help me?"

She fisted my hair and yanked my teeth into her skin. "I made you the Alpha."

I pressed my teeth into the frantic pulse in her neck. It'd be so easy to end her right now. But I needed answers. Answers only she could give. "How, pretty wolf, how? You can tell your future mate."

She giggled. "I took out the Alpha. I made it so you'd be Alpha."

My teeth clamped down on their own will. I battled the beast to end her life and raised my head. A tiny trickle of blood dripped from her neck. *What had I done?*

"Don't you see how perfect we are for each other?"

Her eyes glittered with crazy. I always grasped there was something off about Eloise.

"Thank you," I whispered, and twisted her hands behind her back.

"Kinky. Are you tying me up to have your way with me?"

I tugged a pair of handcuffs from my back pocket and slapped them on her wrists before I broke her arms. She purred in arousal. I grimaced and shoved her away. Turned to the bushes and vomited.

Arrow strode from the trees in human form.

"You all right, buddy?"

"No." I scrubbed the back of my hand over my mouth. "You heard her confession?"

"Yeah. I got it on the tape recorder."

"What?" Eloise screeched and ran down the track.

I sighed. "Can you get her, please? I can't touch her again."

Arrow chuckled and chased Eloise down. He wasn't gentle in dragging her back to the tavern. We marched her inside, told everyone Eloise attacked the Alpha and played the tape. Angus slapped the bar, leaped over it, and took a swing at Eloise. I yanked her back before he ripped her head off. My wolf agreed with him and I'd almost done the same, but logic held. He was a lot easier to deal with since we'd mated with our mate.

"Angus, stand down. She's going to jail. When the Alpha wakes, he'll decide her punishment."

"We should kill her now." He grunted.

"That would make us as bad as her."

A slight smile tugged at his lips. "Your dad will be proud." He returned to behind the bar muttering obscenities under his breath.

Arrow and I shuffled Eloise out the door, into the back of my truck, and drove her into town to the jail cell. She cried and pleaded the entire way, but she'd done this to herself. Who did she think she was coming to our pack and trying to kill the Alpha? She was damn lucky I didn't let Angus rip her head off and toss her body to the pack to rip to shreds. Even luckier I didn't rip her throat out.

It was what she deserved.

After I told Ma what had transpired, I'd have a hard time persuading her to wait until Dad woke before Eloise's punishment would be decided. The night was a long way from over.

CHAPTER EIGHTEEN
BRIANA

SAOIRSE BLEW HER HAIR off her face. "That was a strong one."

I soothed her round stomach. Her contractions had come on hard and fast. "'Tis too soon."

"I know." Tears filled her eyes. She typed another message into the small black device.

"Still no answer?"

"No. What could Arrow be doing as to not answer me?"

"There's important pack business happening."

Saoirse threw the covers off the bed.

"Where do you think you're going?" I helped her to stand.

"I need to go to the waterfall."

"The waterfall?"

"Aye. He's telling me we need to be there. My power is convincing me we need to be there for the birth. It's where I'm happiest, most content. The most at home here on Earth besides with Arrow."

I frowned. "Isn't it a bit of a trek through the forest in the dark?"

"'Tis not that far."

"Saoirse." I sighed.

"Briana, trust me. The lake is pleasant, but you haven't been to the waterfall to feel the power there."

"Power?" I perked up. "What power? Do you think it's the source of our Spring Baile?"

"No. It's not the source."

"Are you sure?"

She shook her head and worried her lip. "Everything is different here. Maybe Father was right. Maybe I should head home to have the baby."

I gasped. "No. You can't leave your mate. You can't take your baby from him."

She wiped her forehead. "I want the baby to live."

"He will." I wrapped a hand around her waist. "Let's go to this waterfall if you think it's the place to give birth, then we need to listen to your power. This baby will have immense power as all royals do, especially a boy. You'll need all the help you can get."

"Way to settle my nerves." She pinched my arm.

"Ow. You wait until you're up to sparring." We walked to the front door. "I'm going to beat your ass with my staff."

We walked toward the door.

"I'd like to see your staff beat my water sword."

I laughed. Sledge had taught me to lighten a grave situation with laughter. My heart thudded for him. I could use his strength now, but he always told me I was strong. I'd be the strongest sister I could be for Saoirse and if the birth didn't end well ... then I'd be stronger still for her. I wouldn't think like that though. Her baby would live. If I thought it, it would happen. Once outside the house, I used my power to part the leaves and branches as we made our way with slow steps into the dense forest of eucalyptus trees.

"I love this scent." Saoirse inhaled. "I'll always associate it with Arrow."

"Sledge's fur holds a tang of the trees."

"You've fallen in love with him?"

"Aye."

"They're easy to love. These wolf shifters are so intriguing, thoughtful, and caring too."

"They love family as much as us. I told Sledge about Donagh and Deirdre."

"How did he take it?" She stopped, placed her hands on her knees, and puffed through another contraction.

"Very well." I massaged her back. "He encouraged me to remember the good times instead of how they died."

"Aw, Sledge is a softie."

"He is, but don't tell him I told you."

Saoirse's contraction stopped, she straightened, blowing out a long breath. We made our way through the forest again.

"Have you told him you love him? You let him mark you so he must know, but have you told him?"

"No. The words are elusive to the both of us."

"We need to duck through those bushes to get to the waterfall." She pointed at a gap in the base of the bushes.

"I'll use my power, so you don't have to bend over." I brandished my glowing hands at the bushes, but they refused to part. "What?" I let go of Saoirse and brushed my hand over the bushes. "Magic."

Saoirse grabbed her stomach and squatted.

"Saoirse." I rushed behind her and held her upright.

She panted hard and sagged against me.

"There's only one way in. We need to go through the small gap." She pointed at the narrow space between the bushes.

I frowned at the opening. What was the magic surrounding this place? Who put it here? And why was there an opening to get in if the place was protected? Protected from what? Or whom? So many questions whirled in my head. Saoirse grabbed my hand and squeezed as another contraction took hold.

"I need in there now." Saoirse ducked through the bushes.

I followed her through the magic and into the enchantment of the waterfall. Water trickled over a rock face into a pool of turquoise alight with thousands upon thousands of fireflies. So reminiscent of the Summer Court. Around us, magic hummed protecting this special place.

"What is this place?"

"Arrow calls it Sona's Waterfall." She lifted her dress over her head and waded into the water. A deep sigh left her lips.

"Waterfall of happiness." I glanced around. "Magic protects this place. Did you not feel it?"

She shook her head. "It was the power in the water I concentrated on."

"You and your love of water."

She used her power to swirl the water to jumping over her head. Another contraction tightened her body forcing her to stop playing with her powers. I waded into the water in my dress and gathered her in my arms.

"How's the baby now?" I asked.

"He's good." She rested her head back on my shoulder. "He loves it here. Ah, here comes another one."

"Already? Shite, do you need to push?"

Saoirse huffed and nodded her head.

"Let's go over to the ledge under the waterfall." I dragged Saoirse through the water and helped her onto the ledge.

The waterfall poured over our heads in a gentle stream of water. So soothing it was like a caress on our bodies. It almost felt like Mother was here brushing our hair back from our faces.

"All right. Pull your legs up and hold on to them tight. Next contraction, you're going to go with the urge to push and push as hard as you can."

Saoirse followed my instructions, and I shuffled between her legs. A bright shock of white was my first sight of the baby.

"He's close, Saoirse."

"Dia." She dug her fingers into her legs and pushed with the next contraction.

The baby's head crowned and pushed out. Saoirse screamed.

"Hold it in. This is the easy part."

"Easy?" She glared at me.

"Aye. When the shoulders come through the royal Fae power will pass into his body from yours and it'll feel like he's ripping you in two."

"He already is." She grumbled. "Briana, I can't do this."

I slapped her face. "Suck it up. You're doing this."

She stroked her cheek. "You're so harsh."

I shrugged.

"I want Arrow." She sobbed as the next contraction took hold.

"Push. Push. Push."

Saoirse pushed. My power hummed in my hands. Saoirse's hands glowed. The waterfall ran faster but was more soothing. The baby glowed in a rainbow of colors. I grinned. A royal birth. So beautiful and special. All the power of the Fae people rolled into one little being. I cradled the baby's head while Saoirse screamed, and pushed, screamed, and pushed. This moment dragged as the Fae power rippled between mother and son, pouring all the strength into the little body. And then his feet slipped free.

I placed the baby on Saoirse's stomach.

"Place your palms on him. One on his head, one on his heart and send your power into him."

"He's not breathing," she screeched.

"Your power now, Saoirse. Donna make me slap you again."

Her palms flared with a rainbow of colors as she accessed all the Fae royal powers for the first time in her life. The baby's little body lit up, and he floated off her stomach into the air snapping the umbilical cord. The fireflies descended and circled the glowing royal baby. He opened his mouth and let out the sweetest cry any new mother could hear.

I swallowed the knot in my throat. "Call your power back now. 'Tis accomplished."

Saoirse's hands stopped glowing, but the baby hovered in the air for a few seconds longer before drifting to her breast and nuzzling on her nipple. Saoirse stoked his little face with a trembling hand.

"He's so little and perfect," she said in absolute awe.

"He is." I eased Saoirse's legs down. "He's strong." I placed a hand on his little back. The next Fae royal. Mother and Father needed to know he was here. They needed to appreciate the power humming through his veins. Our brothers and sisters needed to understand they had a nephew who looked the spitting image of all of us.

Saoirse cried silent tears.

"Why are you crying?" I brushed her tears away.

"I wanted this for so long. I never thought it would happen," she whispered.

My stomach clenched at my sister's pain. Having a baby was the utmost of euphorias. I wouldn't focus on the devastation of losing one. I'd celebrate this moment with my sister.

The fireflies faded with the rising of the sunlight. Saoirse and I sat on the ledge, absorbed in this special moment for what seemed like an eternity.

Arrow emerged through the bushes. "Saoirse," he called and waded into the water.

"Arrow," Saoirse cried again, tears trailing down her cheeks. "He's here."

"So I see." He gathered his family into his arms. "Hey, little guy. Nice to finally meet you."

The baby opened his eyes and peered at his father. Blue and indigo-rimmed eyes. A true Fae royal. Whatever wolf shifter gene Arrow passed onto the baby; it wasn't in looks.

"He looks like you, honey," Arrow said.

"He's strong like you." Saoirse handed Arrow the baby. "What are we naming him?"

"Whatever you want."

"How about Ailbhe?"

I laughed. "After the saint raised by wolves?"

"Perfect." Arrow placed Ailbhe in Saoirse's arms and scooped them both up into his arms. "Let's get you both home."

"Aye. Thank you, my mate."

"My pleasure, my love."

I brushed the tears gathering in the corners of my eyes and strode from the water. I froze at the sight of Sledge standing guard at the entrance with an uncertain look on his face. Were we in danger? Or was it something else?

Arrow placed Saoirse on her feet. Took the baby while Saoirse slid her dress back on.

"I'll go first and make sure it's safe." He disappeared through the bushes.

Saoirse handed the baby to Sledge. "Say hello uncle."

Sledge cradled the tiny baby in his enormous arms. A look of total awe poured from his expressive face. Saoirse disappeared through the bushes.

"He's so tiny," Sledge said and gazed at me. "And the smell. Sweeter than anything I've ever scented."

A knowing smile twitched at my lips while pain lanced my heart.

Sledge ducked through the bushes with the baby safe in his arms. I followed behind. Regret sat like a stone in my stomach I'd never give Sledge a baby of his own and let him gaze at his offspring in awe. Sledge handed Saoirse the baby and Arrow scooped them both up into his arms again and set off through the forest.

I paused at the edge of the bushes surrounding the waterfall instead of following my sister.

Sledge raised an eyebrow. He took one look at my face and the smile fell from his face. "You're leaving."

"Aye," I said.

"She'll want you to stay."

"I know." He didn't say he wanted me to stay. "I need to tell my family about the baby. They deserve to know."

Sledge snorted. "Your father kicked her out."

I shot my gaze to the ground. *Would Father kick me out too if he realized I'd let a wolf shifter mate with me?*

"How long will you be away?" he asked.

"I don't know. Time is different in the Summer Court."

"Are you telling Saoirse before you leave?"

"No. 'Tis best to not upset her. She'll be busy with the baby, anyway."

Sledge clenched his fists. The first sign my leaving upset him.

"I realize I've just accepted us, but I'll be back. I promise," I said and stepped forward to wrap my arms around him.

"Wait." He held his hands up and stopped me. "I did something wrong. I wasn't going to tell you, but it's burning my insides to pieces."

"What did you do?" I curled my fingers into my palms. I knew there was something wrong the second I saw him at the entrance.

He paced away, picked up a fallen branch, and snapped it in two. I frowned. *Why was he so upset?*

He leaned against a tree not meeting my gaze. "I, fuck, I..."

Silence poured from him. A kookaburra laughed in a tree nearby. His laugh was more evil than humorous. I blinked. Sledge's stance, his unwillingness to let me touch him, and guilt, pointed to one thing.

"You were with another woman." The words were like acid in my mouth.

"Not in the way you think, but I did things that make me feel sick."

"Was it Jessa?" I whispered.

"What? No. It wasn't anything like that." He shoved off the tree and finally met my gaze. "I flirted with Eloise to get her to confess to attacking Dad."

"She confessed?" My eyebrows rose.

"Yeah. She's locked in a jail cell right now."

"I'm glad you found your dad's attempted murderer," I said crossing my arms over my damp dress. Sledge's hesitation worried me though. "I understand you flirting with her. I don't like it, but I understand."

"That's not all." He stepped forward, his hands out as though begging me to hear him out.

I stepped back. "Donna touch me until I hear it all."

He dropped his hands to his side. "I placed my arm around her."

My gaze ran over his arms. The arms which held me with such affection. My stomach revolted at the thought of another woman in his arms.

"And?" I whispered.

"I touched my lips to her neck."

Flayed. That's how I suffered. Like whips were striking my body. I stumbled back a step.

Sledge spat on the ground. "No matter what I do, I can't get her horrible taste off my lips. I'm sorry, Briana."

"You planned this. That's why you didn't tell me. You knew I'd never be okay with you touching and kissing another woman."

"I did." He gripped the sides of his head. "I didn't kiss her."

It should make it better but he'd had his mouth on her body.

"I did." He gripped the sides of his head. "I wanted to protect my family in the fastest way I knew how. I knew Eloise wanted me and I used that to my advantage. Please don't hate me."

Sadness seeped from my heart. "I'd never hate you, Sledge. You're my mate."

"There's one more thing I have to tell you before I spend the rest of my life begging for your forgiveness."

I gasped. "You had sex with her?"

"No. Gods, no." He let go of his head. "Worse. I touched my teeth to her neck."

"You bit another woman?" I cried.

He scrambled forward and dropped to his knees. "I wanted her confession. I pretended I'd mark her, but when she confessed, I was angry. My wolf was so enraged he wanted to rip her throat out. I tasted blood before I stopped myself from ending her life."

"She wears your teeth marks?" I gripped his jaw in a tight grip. "Your teeth are mine. How could you do something so intimate with someone else?"

He shut his eyes.

"Sledge," I said, shaking his head. "Do you care so little about us?"

His eyes snapped open. "I love you, Briana."

"You love me?" I released my hold on his face. "This is not love. I had love, and it was beautiful, we would never have betrayed the other the way you did."

"Bree." He stood rising to his full height and commanding presence. "I'm an alpha wolf. They made me alpha of the pack. I needed to put the pack's needs first."

I poked him in the chest. "You wormed your way through my defenses." I poked him again. "You made me care about you and now..." I poked him with a flare of my power. My power demanded to mark him as mine. Then he'd never touch another woman again no matter the reasoning. "I'm going home to the Summer Court." I turned my back on him and walked into the forest.

"Bree, wait."

"What?" I stopped but didn't turn around.

"I promise I'll make this up to you." He walked up behind me. "I promise I'll show you how much I love you." His warm breath skated across the top of my hair. "I promise to adore you from this moment on and do nothing like that again."

My chest heaved. I longed to have him hold me and promise me all those things and to mean them, but he'd opened my heart to love again, and then burned me. I walked away. Not looking back. For if I looked back, it would be the end of my resolve to leave. More important than me and Sledge was the birth of a new Fae royal.

CHAPTER NINETEEN
BRIANA

T HANKFULLY, THE ATRIUM WAS empty on my arrival through the veil into the Summer Court. The once abundance of flowers was never more apparent than after my time away. Once upon a time, the atrium had flourished with flora. My power itched to restore what once was, but it would only last for a fleeting moment in time. I longed to rest on the smooth rocks by the waters edge. To soak in the comfort of our Spring of life. The calming nature of being home in the palace once more. I hadn't thought I'd miss the place but I had. I'd missed my family too.

The quiet trickle of the water into the pool was nothing like the waterfall back in Crystal Creek. There had to be something about the place on Earth that was special. Otherwise, why would there be magical protection around it? If I hadn't been so intent on running back home, I would have investigated it further, but that was the last thing I was thinking about after Sledge's confession.

I slunk through the great marble halls to my bedroom, showered, and dressed in a tight button-up dress to cover Sledge's bite mark on the back of my neck. My hair would cover it anyway, but I was now even more protected by the dress. Afterward, I wound my way through the halls. *Where was everyone?* I required to get them together in one room. There was one way to achieve the task. I walked through the palace to the kitchen.

Grier, the royal family's longest living aide stood from the table. "My lady." He bowed.

"Grier, can you arrange for the family to be present in the dining room for dinner tonight?"

"With pleasure, my lady." He bowed again. "It will be an honor to arrange for you all to dine together again."

I pursed my lips. "All but Saoirse."

He shuffled his feet then clapped his hands at the cook aides. "Right, let's get this feast organized."

The cook aides bustled into action with smiles on their faces as though they'd been waiting for this day. I left the kitchen, a small part of me happy at least I'd strived to bring my family back together. I wandered down to the gallery where paintings of all the royals hung and stopped before my grandparents. They peered on from the depths of their painted gazes with serene guidance. The way I remembered them, always happy together, always taking everything in their stride. Even when they'd burned at the stake, they'd been together.

Together forever as mates.

I progressed to the painting of my former mate Donagh. His intense green eyes stared down at me from under the thick fall of his flaming red hair. He'd been so full of passion and life. So determined to set things right for all of us after I'd almost died. I ran a finger along the lines of his face. The heartache and anger I'd carried for so long since his death no longer lived within me because of Sledge. My new mate. It was unfathomable I'd have two in my life. But I did.

"Donagh," I whispered. I'd loved him. So long ago. I almost forgot what love was like. Until Sledge. "How do I forgive him?"

Quietness met my question. 'Twasn't like I expected an answer.

I moved on to the painting beside him. Our daughter. Deirdre. She was the image of a Fae royal. Silvery-blonde hair. Blue eyes with the indigo ring. Her attitude had been all her fathers. How I'd loved her. My heart still ached with every beat she was no longer by my side. I took small comfort her grandparents and father were with her in the afterlife.

Reaching out a finger, I touched her delicate face, and for the first time in many moons, I didn't shed a tear. I remembered her feisty spirit, the way she'd always wanted me to watch her run and play and chase fireflies through the forest at night or butterflies during the day. How she'd loved trying to tame a unicorn. The majestic creatures never fell for her attempts. They'd allow her to pat them but that was all.

The loud gong of the dinner bell shook me out of my trance. I left the gallery for the dining hall. The entire family sat at the long, formal timber table. Grier had performed his duty.

"Briana, where have you been?" Father stood at the head of the table.

Mother, seated to his right, placed her palm on his arm and he sat down.

"Thank you all for joining me in here tonight." I stood behind my seat. "'Tis been a long time since we all ate together, and this is a momentous occasion. One to be celebrated. Saoirse has birthed the newest Fae royal. A new prince."

"Yes." Ciara sprung up from her seat and hugged me.

Mother placed her hands over her mouth. Father glowered. Rian grinned. So did Lorcan. Aislinn stabbed her fork into the table, and Roisin clapped her hands.

"He is well?" Mother asked.

"His birth was spectacular. As all Fae royal births are. I wish you'd been there, Mother."

She scrubbed tears from her eyes. Father whispered in her ear and hugged her.

I cleared my throat. "Father, please allow Saoirse to come home where she belongs. The new prince will need us."

"No." He slammed his hands on the dining table. "She made her choice, and she chose her mate."

"Saoirse mated?" Roisin asked.

"Aye, to a wolf shifter," I said.

"A what?" Roisin asked. "How? Aren't we meant to mate with Fae?"

"Precisely," Father said.

"Mating is not so simple, Father." I sat in my chair. My legs growing unsteady with the notion he'd kick me out of the Summer Court if he knew of my mating with a wolf shifter too. "We don't choose who we are fated with."

Mother placed her hand on his arm again. "She's right."

He placed his hand over hers. "I've fought so hard to keep you all safe. I won't have you prancing around on Earth, leaving yourself open to attack."

"Saoirse appeared quite safe with the wolf shifters. They protect their town with magic," I said. "They are a family like ours and they'll protect her and the new prince when you won't."

Father's face flickered with emotions as his crown wreathed around his head. "I can't believe you went to Earth too. After everything you lost, I thought you'd be the last to leave the safety of the Summer Court."

"The locked veil is restricting us. Suffocating us." I tugged the collar of my dress. "You made certain there is no threat to us from the Trappers."

Father threw his hands up in the air. "At an enormous cost."

"I intend to visit Saoirse and her son," I said, squaring my shoulders. "I hope you all will make the effort too."

Father glowered. "I can't sit by and watch you put yourself in danger by going to Earth."

He shoved back his chair and strode from the room. So much for smoothing things over. I drew in a deep breath and let it out. Mother hummed quietly as she stared after Father's retreating back. Rian cleared his throat.

"Tell us more about this wolf pack," Lorcan said.

"And Saoirse," Aislinn said.

"And the baby," Ciara said.

"All right." I smiled. At least most of the family was excited about the baby. "Let's eat. This is a celebration of life."

Mother turned her concerned gaze after Father back to us and raised her glass. "To the new prince."

We all raised our glasses and toasted. Together, as a family, we welcomed the new prince into the royal family. One day they'd all meet him. I'd make sure they did for Saoirse needed her family as much as we needed her, and the future of the royals now lay at her feet. For if she gave birth to one baby, then she'd have another baby the next time she was in heat.

Many moons later, I'd stayed in the Summer Court, even though I'd told everyone all there was to know about Saoirse. They hungered for every detail. Especially Mother. Father avoided me like he knew I'd tell him something he didn't want to realize.

That I'd also mated to a wolf shifter.

So we both pretended I was the same. It worked. For now. The longer I was away from Sledge, the more I desired to see him. To hold him. To have him hold me, but the pain of his betrayal still scorched my heart.

I wandered through the rose garden. More a field of rose bushes. The heady scent of the ever-flowering blooms in an array of pinks and reds rustled in the slight breeze. I stroked my fingers against the silky soft petals and inhaled their sweet aroma.

"Briana." Roisin waved through the expanse of rose bushes and made her way to me.

"Good morning."

"This is my favorite place to be at the start of the day. The way the dewdrops cling to the blooms with the rising of the sun warming the flowers into a potent floral sweetness. It's poetic."

I threaded my arm through hers. "You're the poet."

"I try." She ducked her head. A small flower from her crown fell to the ground and mingled with the fallen rose petals. "What is troubling you?"

"Are you looking for inspiration for your next poem?"

"Mayhap." She smiled. "Broken hearts make for a fascinating poem."

"What makes you think I have a broken heart?"

"Small things. You gaze off into the distance without seeing what you're looking at. You sigh long and deep like the pain inside must escape. When you talk about the wolf shifters, your eyes light up with love. There was more to your time with Saoirse."

"You're too observant." I frowned.

"What is his name?"

"Sledge."

"Sledge? 'Tis a strange name."

"It's his nickname. His name is Sheldon."

"I suppose he wanted a more masculine name?"

"I'd say so. He's a big wolf shifter. Sheldon doesn't fit him. Sledge does."

She paused and picked a bright crimson rose. "Do you love him?"

"I fell in love with him."

"Another Fae princess mated to a wolf shifter. What are the odds? Things are changing, Briana, changing for the better, I hope. Why are you here if you love him?"

"He hurt me."

"How?" Her power flared into her hands with a rapid display. "I'll return the favor."

I chuckled at her young impetuousness. "He touched another woman in a way a mate should never do."

"Have you marked him?"

"No, but he's still my mate. He marked me. He made me fall in love with him."

Roisin laughed. "He can't make you fall in love with him. Only you can do that. Your love is yours to give."

"Hush, you're too young to be so smart."

"Does he love you? What am I saying? Of course, he does. You're the mighty Briana. So strong and capable. I wish I was as strong as you. Did he have a reason to touch this woman? Did you kill her with your staff? Decapitate her?"

"No, I didn't kill her." I dipped my head. "Have you been sparring with Father?"

"Aye." She grinned. "Lorcan and Aislinn too. So did he?"

"Aye. He stated a reason to protect his family. A valid reason now I've had the distance to think about it. But he should still not have touched her. He should have found another way."

"And if it was you he protected. Would you forgive him for touching another woman then?"

"I don't know."

"If you were about to burn at the stake and he could stop it by touching a woman. What would you say?"

I rubbed my wrists. "Low blow, Roisin."

"Answer the question," she demanded.

"I'd tell him to do anything to stop me burning." I rubbed my wrists harder. How I longed for the comfort of Sledge's hands to take the pain in my wrists away. "I better hear this poem you're about to write about me."

Roisin grinned. "You will. One day." She skipped off through the rose bushes betraying her younger age in the action. Yet her words had been so grown up. Family. I huffed. They always knew better than you about your life.

This time they might be right.

After Roisin's too astute insights into my love life, I sought out Rian for a sparring match. He was only too eager to appease me.

Rian twirled his staff and grinned. "Any reason you always wear collared dresses since your return?"

I circled Rian twirling my staff. "No."

He stepped forward swinging his staff in a brutal attack. I blocked. He spun with a twirl in the air and slammed his staff down. I held my staff sideways and blocked sending a loud crack of timber on timber through the air. I spun and attacked. He squatted, missing my staff, and swung at my feet with a loud swish through the air of his staff. I jumped high. He charged forward with a jabbing motion and caught me in the stomach. I jerked back with a grunt.

Rian grinned. "You're off your game. You'd never let me get you with that swing."

I brushed my hair off my face and spun my staff. He was right. Seemed everyone was these days. I used my power to disintegrate his staff.

Rian laughed.

I dissolved my staff and stomped out of the courtyard.

"Briana, wait up."

"What?"

"Saoirse was as cagey as you when she returned from Earth last time."

"I'm not Saoirse." I strode through the great marble halls. After my talk with Roisin that morning, I was a mess of churning emotions, and I needed the peace of the Spring Baile. As depleted as it was, it still healed.

"Dia, sisters can be difficult." He huffed following me.

I turned into the atrium and made my way across the cobblestones. By the pool, I knelt on a boulder and dragged my fingers in the water. The once abundant supply of plant life and glorious display of flowers had dwindled too. I used my power to add new green leaves and flowers to the plants.

Rian ran a hand over one of the new flowers. "I sometimes wish I had one great power like yours."

I jerked my hand free of the water. "Why?"

"You produce life where it's depleted or where there is none."

He sat alongside me. Sadness crept into his eyes. That night damaged all of us.

"Rian, do you think it's acceptable for leaders to do what's necessary for the safety of their people?" I raised my knees and placed my chin on them.

"Father does what he thinks is right to keep us safe. We understand that."

"Aye. I meant any leader. Not just Father."

A darkness passed over his face. "Yes."

I slanted my head and studied his face, but he said nothing else.

"One of us should go to Earth and visit Saoirse soon," I said.

"I thought you'd head back since Father doesn't seem to have a problem with you flitting back and forth between Earth and the Summer Court. If you watch out for Saoirse, we can keep looking for the source of the spring."

I released my knees. "Did I tell you about the waterfall where Saoirse gave birth?"

"You did."

"And the surrounding magic?"

"Magic? You didn't mention magic."

I massaged my forehead. "I thought I did. What do you think it means? Why would someone put a magic protection around a waterfall?"

Rian shrugged. "It could be the Water Sprites. Could be witches or anything. I'll have to look closer at the forest."

"Yes."

I'd look closer too. Perhaps it was as simple as a protection for the wolf shifters like the one around their town. But what if it was more? My cheeks heated. I placed my palms on my face. Why was I hot all of a sudden? A tingle of awareness slithered down my spine like it did when I was near Sledge, but he was nowhere near me. My heart picked up speed.

"Ah." I stood. No, not now. I couldn't be coming into heat this quick. I didn't have any telltale signs. Or did I? And I'd ignored them to focus on my broken heart?

Rian's nostrils flared. "You don't have heats anymore."

I ran from the atrium to my bedroom. I rushed through the door and dropped to my hands and knees. Under the bed, I knocked the lid off the tiny compartment in the base of my bed.

"Briana, what are you doing?" Rian asked following me once more.

The small glass vial fell from the compartment, but instead of landing in my palm, as it often did, it missed my shaking hand and landed on the floor with a loud crack and breaking of glass.

"No," I cried as the amethyst-colored liquid spilled onto the floor.

Rian yanked me from under the bed. "What's going on?"

"Shut the door." I shoved him away.

He closed my bedroom door as I sunk onto my bed.

"I, ah, many years ago I found a witch from our old witch seer Saltine Woodswillow's line to make me a potion to stop my heat." I pointed at the floor. "That was my last potion. I've been unable to find the witch again or anyone from her line."

Rian's mouth dropped open. "Why didn't you say anything?"

"I would have if I'd found her again, but I needed the potions for myself." I twisted my dress in my hands. "You don't understand. You never lost a child. You never lost a baby before it was born. I couldn't go through it anymore. This was my way to stop it."

Rian sunk onto the bed alongside me. "Briana." He sighed. "We would have understood."

"Truly?" I blinked back the tears collecting in my eyes.

"Aye. Are there other witches who can make the potion?"

"I have found none from her line. I think she may have been the last one after the burnings. Although..." I stopped twisting my dress. Pepper Woods had seemed familiar. Was she related to the witch who made my potion? Would she be able to make me more potions? "But I can't go back to Earth and ask."

If I returned, I'd have to ask Sledge to call the witch. If I saw Sledge while in heat, then I'd tie him up and have my way with him again, and again, and again until my heat was over. And then I'd end up pregnant like Saoirse.

"No. I can't."

My body heated even more. Every nerve ending lit with electricity making my skin feel hypersensitive. My stomach clenched. Shite, my heat was here.

Rian fluttered his hand, parting the veil in my bedroom. "You need to leave now before Father realizes you can still produce a baby. 'Tis the reason he hasn't insisted on you choosing a Fae mate inside the Summer Court."

"How did you part the veil here?" I shoved my hands to my aching thighs.

"We can do it anywhere. We're royals, Briana." He shoved me off the bed. "Hurry. Your scent is growing."

I stepped into the shimmering veil and stopped. "Wait, where am I going?"

"Back to Saoirse, of course." He closed the veil to the Summer Court in my face.

I only had one way to go. To Earth, Crystal Creek, and Saoirse. The one place, I wanted and didn't want to go. To Sledge.

CHAPTER TWENTY
SLEDGE

BEING NEAR SAOIRSE AND the baby, was the closest I'd get to Briana. She wasn't coming back any time soon. It'd been months. Dad woke a few weeks after she left and I'd impressed him with the way I'd run the pack, and how I'd discovered Eloise attempt to kill him. How I'd put her in jail and left her fate to him. He'd decided to keep her in prison. Life in a cage was worse than death for a wolf shifter. I sometimes wondered if I should have ripped out her throat or let Angus do it, then I wouldn't have the reminder of how I'd betrayed my mate.

Dad even left me as Alpha. He admitted he was ready for retirement. He'd never be able to retire in completeness, the alpha wolf inside him wouldn't let him, but I didn't mind he'd always have my back in this town I called home. A town and pack I'd give up for Briana. If she'd have me again.

I was busy during the day. I held a new respect for Dad and the amount of work he did to run the pack. But the nights ... the nights were long and lonesome without Briana in the same bed as me stroking my body in either human or wolf form. At this stage, I didn't care so long as I felt her fingers on me again.

I cooed at the tiny boy in my arms. His shock of silvery-white hair another reminder of Briana and what I'd screwed up.

Saoirse smiled from the other side of the couch where Arrow held her in the embrace of his arms.

"Uncle Sledge has a way with babies," she joked for the millionth time.

"Your ma is such a tease." I winked at Arrow.

Arrow threw his head back and laughed. Damn, I'd never seen a happier wolf shifter than I did when I looked at my best friend. Envy ate my stomach.

My head jerked up. The scent. Familiar. Intense. Briana.

Arrow's nose twitched. "Your sister's here."

"Briana?" Saoirse scrambled out of Arrow's arms and raced for the front door.

She yanked it open. Briana stood on the doorstep with her hand elevated in the air ready to knock. The sisters hugged and mumbled, cried, mumbled again. Whispered. Saoirse shot me a glance and whispered again and shut them both outside.

Arrow took Ailbhe from my arms and placed the sleeping baby in his bouncer.

"Shit," Arrow said. He snapped his fingers my face. "You know what this means?"

I curled my lip and snarled.

"Dude, you did not just growl at me with my baby in the room." Arrow folded his arms. "I get it. Your mate's heat scent makes you even wilder."

"Sorry." I stood. "Heat? She can't come near me then."

"What are you on about? She's your mate. You take care of her needs."

"I know, but she hates me for what I did with Eloise. You've seen parts of her past. Do you really think she'd want to get knocked up by a mate she hates?"

He unfolded his arms. "She doesn't hate you. You upset her, but she won't hate you."

"How can you be so sure?"

"Because she's your mate too, so she'll take care of your needs. And let me tell you when Saoirse takes care of my needs..."

I sliced my hand through the air. "I don't need sex talk while I'm inhaling Briana's heat scent."

Arrow laughed and slapped my shoulder.

Saoirse returned through the door. By herself. What the fuck? Did Briana never want to see me again? Did I ruin everything we'd shared?

"Sledge, Briana would like you to call your witch friend and ask her if she can make a potion for her."

"Why didn't she ask me?"

"You understand why." Saoirse lasered her gaze on my face with a hostility I'd never had from her before.

"Fine." Guilt slammed into my chest. I yanked out my phone. "What sort of potion?"

"One to stop her heat."

Right. I dialed Pepper's number. She answered in an instant. Unlike her.

"Pepper, are you able to make a potion to stop a Fae heat?"

"Hello to you too, Sledge."

"Pepper, this is urgent."

Pepper sighed. "How long do I have to make one?"

"She's in heat now."

Pepper cackled. "Too late, dear Sledge. Too late." She cackled again and hung up.

Saoirse stared at me with wide eyes.

"She can't." I shoved my phone into my jeans pocket.

"Shite," Saoirse said. "I guess you should head home."

"I'm not going anywhere without talking to my mate," I said meeting her glare head-on. There was no way I wouldn't talk to Briana, not when she'd been away so long and now she stood outside the house.

Arrow scooped Saoirse into his arms. "Honey, you can't stop whatever is about to happen."

"She's my sister."

"And Sledge is her mate. He'll take care of her."

Saoirse met Arrow's pointed look then nodded her approval. I walked to the front door and inhaled the fervent odor of Briana in heat. My mouth watered.

Keep it together, buddy.

My wolf snapped. Growled. Paced.

There was only one way I'd keep him in check, and that was to knock his ass out. It was the perfect solution, and the only way Briana and I would make it together. I needed to show her I'd put her first.

I swung open the door and strode outside.

Briana sprang from the swing seat. "Can Pepper make a potion?"

"No. I'm sorry."

Briana's gaze dragged down my chest and raked my body. Her scent grew stronger. I shoved my hands in my pockets to stop myself from reaching for my mate and devouring her body like a crazed beast.

"I missed you," I said.

She shuddered. "Sledge, I can't do this now. All I can think about is sex. And having you so close..." She stepped closer and raised her hands to my chest.

She ran her warm palms over my muscles. I'd longed for Briana's touch while she was in the Summer Court, but not like this. Not when I didn't know if she'd forgiven me. But I could take care of my mate's needs. As I should have before.

"Let me take care of you." I inhaled her ripe aroma and dug my nails into my palms. "Ask me to touch you, Bree."

"Aye. Touch me, Sledge."

I placed my hands over hers and lured her to my truck affording us a small amount of privacy. I opened the back door and hoisted her onto the seat. She dragged me to her. A long moan left her lips as my body covered hers.

"Sweetheart." I thrust my hands onto the seat and lifted my chest. "You have to realize how sorry I am I hurt you."

"Sledge." She tugged my shirt from my jeans. "I do."

"Do you forgive me?" Her forgiveness meant more to me than the pack and my family. She was my family. Everything we were together and would be was more important than anything else. I should have realized that. I was a dumbass.

"Aye," she whispered. "Aye, my mate."

A shudder wracked my body. "Say that again."

"My mate."

I smiled. "I've longed for you to say those words. Mark me, Bree."

"Now?" She pouted.

I stroked the side of her face. "Now. Right this moment. Mark me as yours."

"What about the pack? Are you still Alpha?"

"Yes, but you're what's important. I'll always put you and your needs first. As I should have before."

Her eyes softened, and she pressed a soft kiss to my lips. My lips lingered against hers feeling the forgiveness in the barest of touches between our lips.

"I'm in heat. I need you," she whispered against my lips.

"We can't. I can't." I moved back and ran my finger across her lips. Lips I wanted to ravage with passion. "As much as I want you any time, and as hard as I am for you with your heat scent, I can't have sex with you."

She hooked her legs around my waist and rolled her hips. She sucked in a breath then puffed out, "Why?"

"You understand why." I kissed her forehead. "You're in heat. If we have sex, you'll end up pregnant."

"I ..." Her eyes glistened with tears.

"It's okay, sweetheart. You're not ready. I'm a patient wolf shifter when it comes to you, and we'll have all the time in the world once you mark me."

"Aye." She unbuttoned my shirt and ran her hands over my chest. Her hips rolled again. Her scent almost made me lose control. She rocked against me harder.

I ground my hips into her.

Briana moaned. Her palms glowed. Her power grew hotter against my chest.

She wrenched her hands back. "What am I going to do while you're in the Quiet and I'm in heat?"

"Bree. You're strong. Amazing." I tugged her hands to my chest. "You've survived so much, and you'll survive your heat without me. You're a Fae princess. You can do anything."

She rocked her hips. "I don't know if I can."

I rocked with her. Harder. Faster. Rubbing my hard cock against the junction of her legs. The zipper in my jeans too rough for me to enjoy to completion, but Briana enjoyed it, so I'd do this for my mate. For the woman I loved.

"Mark me while you come against me." I grabbed her legs and tilted her hips.

"Aye." She gasped.

"That's the spot, isn't it?" I ground against her.

Her palms glowed against my chest. I gritted my teeth against the power surging into me.

"That's it, sweet thing. Keep going. Make me yours."

She lost herself to the rhythm of my hips. Her pants grew faster. She was close. So close. And I wanted more than anything to feel her around my cock, but I'd do anything for Briana, and preventing her from becoming pregnant was the best thing for her right now. We still had so much to talk about. I still had to grovel and make it up to her.

Once I woke from the Quiet after absorbing Briana's memories, I'd make it my mission to do anything she wanted.

Her palms grew hotter. Her memories slipped into my head. So many it hurt. I pumped my hips faster as I started slipping into the darkness. I had to take care of my mate first. Her power scorched my chest right over my heart. Into my heart.

She cried out with her release. A surge of her power zapped my flesh.

My vision blackened, and then I was no longer aware of my mate under my body, all I was aware of was her memories. The smiling face of her daughter fluttered into view. My heart broke for Briana to lose her.

"Sledge, don't you stay away long," were the last words I heard before the Quiet took me on its journey of Briana's memories.

CHAPTER TWENTY-ONE
BRIANA

S LEDGE'S BODY WAS HEAVY on top of mine, and not in a good way. The Quiet claimed him while the mark I inflicted on his chest glowed brightly before fading to a swirl of dark knots over his heart.

He was mine now. He'd always been mine. I'd just been too scared to mark him. Yet, now I had, the last few months seemed ridiculous. My fears, my jealousy, my unwillingness to move on were things of the past. Sledge was mine, as I was his. I wriggled out from under his hefty weight. Dia, the wolf shifter was massive. With a few more huff and puffs, I made it out of the truck. I couldn't very well leave Sledge here for whoever knew how long he'd be in the Quiet.

Fae mating left a lot to be desired, in particular when you were in heat. I suppose it was why Fae mating with a Fae was preferable so you'd both go to the Quiet at the same time. I straightened my dress, made my way to the front door and knocked.

Saoirse flung the door open like she'd been standing on the other side waiting for me.

"Are you all right?" She ran her gaze over me.

"I'm in heat, Saoirse. No, I'm not all right." I crossed my arms.

She smirked. "I meant with Sledge."

"Aye, I forgave his stupid ass." I uncrossed my arms and pointed at the truck. "I marked him. Can Arrow move him from the truck?"

Arrow strode over from rocking the baby in the bouncer. "Sure. Where do you want him? Here or at his house?"

"I, ah, would here be too much of an inconvenience? I'd like to visit with you and watch over Sledge."

"Done." Arrow strode outside.

"Come inside," Saoirse said. "Your nephew wants a cuddle."

I placed my hands over my chest to smother the pounding excitement of my heart.

Saoirse led me to the contented baby, picked him up, and placed him in my arms.

I swallowed. "Saoirse, he's perfect."

"Aye. He is." She smiled with all the love she held for her baby.

"What the ever-loving fuck, Briana?" Arrow strode into the house with Sledge cradled in his arms.

"What?" *Was he upset I held Aibhle?* I'd never harm their baby.

"You marked Sledge while he's sporting a boner? The damn thing poked me in the stomach when I hoisted him over my shoulder. No best friend should ever have to go through that."

Saoirse giggled. I placed a hand over my mouth.

Arrow stomped down the hallway and vanished into the bedroom I'd once stayed in. Guess I was back to listening to Arrow and Saoirse having sex all the time. As if my heat couldn't get any worse.

"You're harsh, Briana," Saoirse said. "How is everyone back home?"

"Come, sit down and I'll tell you everything. They all miss you, and they were all happy to hear about the new prince."

"All except Father," she said with too much perception into our family.

"He wasn't unhappy." I sat on the couch. "He'll come around one day."

"I doubt it." She sat by my side.

I held her hand. Sisterly love was what she needed, and while I was here, sisterly love was what I'd give her.

"What are you going to do while you're in heat?" she asked.

I shrugged. "Nothing."

She sucked in a breath. "If you'll watch Aibhle, Arrow and I will make sure not to have sex in the house while you're in heat."

"Deal." If only she'd carry that over after my heat finished.

A day's reprieve was good though. A day of this insane sexual hunger and no relief. I could do that. Maybe. I brushed a hand through my hair, catching my fingers on my flower crown. I hoped Sledge was right, and I was strong enough. The pressure of my heat built to a peak again. I rocked the baby and concentrated on talking to Saoirse about home and the family. As good a distraction as I'd find. Her baby might keep me sane for the next day.

Almost a week later, after I'd barely survived my heat without rubbing myself against Sledge's rock-hard erection, I paced the room with Aibhle, who cried in hunger. Saoirse and Arrow had ventured to their favorite place the waterfall. I supposed they'd lost track of time while enjoying each other.

"Shh." I patted the baby's back and paced into my bedroom where Sledge still rested in the Quiet. "Your mother will be back soon." I stepped over to the window, brushed the curtain back, and peered into the forest. "Come on, Saoirse, how long do you need to have sex for?"

"All day," a rough voice said behind me.

I spun with a start.

Sledge sat up on the bed and gazed at me with such hunger, I almost forgot the crying baby in my arms.

"Give him to me." Sledge held out his enormous hands.

I crossed the small distance and handed Aibhle to Sledge.

"What's the problem, dude?" Sledge placed him on his shoulder and patted his bottom.

"He's hungry."

"I know the feeling. I could go for a big juicy stack of pork ribs with barbeque sauce." Sledge licked his lips.

I wrinkled my nose.

The baby quietened until his cries were little sobs then nothing as he slipped into sleep.

"How did you do that?" I sat on the end of the bed.

"I have the magic touch." He polished his knuckles on his chest then returned to patting the baby's bottom.

How I longed for his touch on me. My body heated from just looking at his hands.

Sledge inhaled and grinned. "How long was I out?"

"'Twas not long. Six days."

"Yeah? Arrow was out for ages."

"Your Alpha wolf would never let you stay down that long," I said.

"You understand me so well." He stopped patting the baby and touched my thigh.

Heat and passion roared through my body from his simple touch.

"And now you know me."

"Please," he scoffed. "I didn't need to see your memories to know you. I already knew you loved blueberries, are an amazing sister, a thoughtful daughter, an exceptional mother, and a passionate mate."

The truth in his words circled my heart. He was right. I'd shared so much of myself with him before we'd marked each other. We'd entwined our hearts even without our mating marks.

"Thank you, for you know." I nodded at the baby.

He inched closer to me. "We weren't ready for this, and if we're not ready next time you're in heat, you'll have to find another way to knock my ass out, because sweetheart, your scent..." He rumbled.

I chuckled. "Pheromones will do that to a man."

"It was more than that for me." He slid his hand between my thighs. "You're the woman I love."

"Oh, Sledge." I placed my hand on top of his. "How do you always say the right words?"

"I can't wait to take you home." He shifted the baby to his other shoulder and nuzzled my hair.

I urged his hand into the junction of my thighs. His fingers stroked the inside of my thigh.

"I'm going to love you all day, and then I'll start all over again."

"Is that right?" I rose my eyebrows. "I'm not in heat anymore."

"Makes no difference to me. I'm so hard for you it's a wonder I can talk."

I laughed and placed my other hand on the bulge in his jeans.

"Sweet thing, you keep that up and we'll be having sex with the baby in the room and Arrow will kick my ass."

"Saoirse too. She's itching for her sword fighting student to get back out there."

The baby woke and wailed again.

Sledge stood. "They're almost here. He must have a wolf shifter's nose."

"Thank the Summer Court." I joined Sledge in meeting Saoirse and Arrow at the front door.

Sledge handed Aibhle to Saoirse.

"You're up," Arrow said.

"Yeah." Sledge wrapped an arm around my waist and urged me through the door. "Thanks for the hospitality. We'll see you in a few days."

Arrow chuckled and slapped Sledge on the back.

"There goes our babysitter," Arrow said.

"Don't worry, your mother will take over," Saoirse said, settling on the couch with the ravenous baby.

Sledge led me to his truck, opened the door for me, and settled me in the seat like I was his most precious cargo. I almost wished I'd fallen pregnant with his baby while in heat just to see him as a doting father. He'd be sweet and caring, protective too. I dipped my head and studied him as he drove home. The notion of having his baby didn't send terror rippling through me. Fear fluttered in my stomach, but I was also intrigued. The next time I was in heat, whenever that occurred, these things were so unpredictable, I wouldn't knock his sexy ass out. I'd embrace our future together as a family.

The truck stopped outside his house. A ripple of homecoming coursed through my heart. I loved the Summer Court, but this house, Sledge, he was my home now. I'd manage going back and forth between the two worlds. As Sledge said, I was a powerful Fae princess, and I could do anything.

He led me inside the house and sat me on his bed. "I worried I'd never see you here again."

The pain in his words rang through my heart. I ran my hands over the fur rug on the end of his massive bed and said, "I missed stroking your fur."

"Later, much later, you can stroke my wolf. But for now, I need your touch on my skin."

"As I need yours." I stood and unbuttoned the high collar of my dress, down the front until I could slip the sleeves from my shoulders and let the material pool at my feet.

Sledge ran his tongue over his lips. "You're so gorgeous."

"Undress for me."

"With pleasure." He unbuttoned his shirt and dropped it on the floor.

I smiled at my mark on his chest. He dropped his gaze to his body then ran a finger over the swirling knots embedded in his skin.

"I sense so much in your mark."

"You'll be able to find me anywhere now."

His gaze jerked to my face. "I can track you through the mark?"

"Aye."

"Damn, that's hot." He smirked and unbuttoned his pants. "My wolf thinks so too."

"Your alpha wolf would track me by my scent, anyway."

"Eh." He kicked his jeans off his feet. "Double the tracking potential. Can't complain about that. On the bed, sweetheart."

I sat on the bed and wriggled up to the headboard. Sledge crawled onto the bed. He kissed my ankle. I squirmed and laughed. He swapped to my other ankle.

"Sledge." I giggled. "What are you doing? That is very ticklish."

"I intend to kiss and lick every inch of your body."

"Even my little toe?" I rose my eyebrow.

He picked my foot up and swiped his tongue around my little toe.

I laughed and tugged my foot free. "Anywhere but my feet, they're too ticklish."

His eyebrows shot into his hair. "How, when you never wear shoes?"

I shrugged and crooked my finger. "Come here."

Sledge crawled over me and whispered in my face, "Here?"

"Aye."

"What do you want me to do here?" He rocked his hips against mine.

"Lower and to the right." I raised my head to kiss him.

He chuckled and slid down my body. "I haven't kissed you and licked you everywhere yet."

His mouth latched onto my nipple. I sunk my hands into his hair. The warm, moist, suction shot a dart of pleasure from my breast to my core. He slid his tongue to the sensitive skin under my breast. His lips kissed a trail down my ribs to my hip bone. My hips jerked at the glowing sensation his lips and tongue were igniting on my body. His mouth traveled lower, across the junction of my thighs, down the inside of my leg, kissing and licking with the occasional suck on my skin into his mouth. Desire licked flames through my body and more, through my heart too.

"Turn over," he demanded with a deep huskiness.

I gave him a seductive smile and rolled over keeping my gaze on his desirable body. Dia, my mate was a stunning specimen of a wolf shifter.

He brushed my hair from my back with soft strokes of his fingers sending prickles of arousal across my skin. His fingers kneaded against the muscles in my neck.

I closed my eyes and moaned.

He massaged my neck until it was boneless then he kissed, licked, and suckled my neck until I moaned with the need for my mate to pleasure me. To sink his teeth into my skin.

"Bite me," I said.

Sledge froze.

I rolled over and cupped his cheeks in both hands.

"I want to." He kissed my lips with my hands still on his cheeks. "I..."

"You still feel guilty?"

"Yes. I never meant it to go that far."" He dropped his forehead to mine.

"I understand," I said, stroking my thumbs against his jaw. "You're a leader. You put others before yourself."

He sat up. "I'll never put anyone before you again. If that means I'm no longer Alpha, then..."

I sighed as I sat up and wrapped my arms around him until my head rested on his chest on my mark.

"You give nothing up." I lifted my chin. "You don't expect me to give up going to the Summer Court."

"Of course not. That's your home, and where most of your family is."

"I don't expect you to give up anything either."

His gaze scanned my face. "You mean that?"

I ran a finger over my mating mark on his body. "This mark ties us together in the way your bite mark did. Every time you bite me, I feel you tying us together even more. Bite me, Sledge."

"Bree." He sighed and brushed my hair from my shoulder.

I shivered in anticipation.

He lowered his head slowly. Kissed his lips to my skin setting a race to my heart. Licked the prickles dancing over my skin. Raked his teeth on my neck. I sucked in a deep breath of longing. Every time he bit me, I felt more his, and I needed that now after making him mine.

I needed to be his.

I wanted to be his.

"Harder." I moaned.

Sledge growled and dug his teeth into my neck.

"Aye," I cried.

He half growled and chuffed. I dug my fingers into his chest. He urged me back onto the bed. I draped my legs around his waist. His fingers trailed down my body to my welcoming dampness. He toyed with my hard nub and released his teeth to lick the now inflamed, sensitive skin. He nibbled across my jaw. His lips met mine. Our tongues thrust and swirled in a ravenous kiss. A kiss that was full of the longing for each other for the last few months apart. And more. From the first moment, we met in the forest and his lips brushed against mine, I'd wanted this.

Sledge kissed me and kissed me. More insistent and demanding than the last. I loved it. I loved him. He may have wanted to show me he loved me with gentle loving, but this, this hard and demanding loving was our way of showing each other. His finger slid into my wet opening. I was so slick and ready for him that my muscles clenched his finger, demanding more. He slid it out and thrust back in, hard and fast until I panted and scratched at his back. The pressure built. His kiss grew frantic. My muscles tightened. My pleasure focused on the one place his finger toyed with me and made me lose my mind.

I came against his hand, gripping the back of his head to hold his lips against mine. His finger swirled inside me rubbing my clenching muscles until the orgasm rippled to an end. I released my hold on his head and smiled.

"You feel amazing when you come."

He lowered his head to my nipple and scraped his teeth over the hard bud.

The sated afterglow vanished with one touch of his teeth. I thrashed my head on the mattress. Sledge made good on his promise. He kissed and licked every inch of my body until I begged him for his cock.

He rolled over onto his back. "Ride me, sweet thing. Let me watch you work my cock into your hot body and come all over me."

I straddled his hips and lowered myself onto his hard cock. I moaned and dipped my chin to my chest. Dia, he was so big and hot, and hard inside me. So mine. I swayed my hips. Sledge grunted. I lifted my chin and met his searing gaze. He blew me a kiss. I rolled my eyes.

"Do that again." He thrust up at the same time as I shoved down.

I grunted, raised my hips, and slammed down with him thrusting up again.

"Yeah, that's it," Sledge said. "Ride me hard."

"Sledge." I slapped my hands to his chest for support as our hips bucked against each other again and again. The slam of his hard cock sliding along my walls hit the very depths of me with a tiny sting of pain. His thumbs found my lower lips and spread me wider around his hard shaft making me even hotter and more turned on.

My breathing turned to pants. He pressed his thumbs to my hard nub. Pleasure shot sparks to everything he was doing to my body even though I was the one riding him. He stroked his thumbs slower, slowed his thrusts. My hips followed his lead even though I was close to release.

"Right there," he said. "That peak before you fall. It's the best place with you knowing I've made you happy."

"You've made me happy in other ways too," I whispered.

Our hips rocked leisurely in time to the slow roll of his thumb on my clit.

"Good. I want to make you happy always."

"Let me come." I thrust my hips. "I'll be happy then."

Sledge smirked. "I'm happy now."

"Glad one of us is." I panted, wound so tight. If he just picked up the pace a fraction...

"I'll always make you happy and if you want to come, then that's what I'll do."

He thrust his cock in and out with an even tempo while his thumb circled my clit. Happiness was here in this place of building tension. My hips slowed as I lost myself to the building pleasure. Sledge took over and made sure every place his cock stroked deep inside me sent a tighter quiver of muscles to my building orgasm. My power rose to my hands. Sledge grunted but kept up his pace. The mark on his chest glowed under my palm.

So perfect and right.

My mate.

Mine.

My orgasm rippled so strong it knocked the oxygen from my lungs. I slammed down on Sledge's cock feeling him buried deep while the pulses of my orgasm rippled along his length making my thighs quiver. Sledge brushed my long hair back from my face as the bliss washed over me.

"Happy?"

"Aye."

"Good," he said. "My mate deserves to be happy." He rolled us over. "Prepare to be happy again."

"Sledge." I laughed then moaned as he pumped his hips.

"Yeah, sweetheart?"

This man, wolf shifter, mate. Even with his own need raging at him, he was taking care of me. He'd take care of me for the rest of our lives.

"I love you," I admitted.

His gaze softened. Love shone back at me, but then it had for a while.

"I love you too, Bree."

I wrapped my legs around his waist. "Make me happy again."

"Always." He kissed me, all teeth and tongue, hardness and passion. The way I loved him most. And I'd love him the way he was forever.

EPILOGUE

A FEW DAYS AND many orgasms later, Sledge and I explored the outer ring of trees and bushes around the waterfall. There was something niggling me about this place. The way Saoirse and the baby loved it. The way magic protected it.

"I don't feel any magic," Sledge said.

I swept my hand over the bushes and trees. "I do. If the wolf shifters didn't ask witches to put this protection barrier here, then who did?"

"And why?" Sledge frowned.

"Good question." I called my power to my hands and tried to manipulate the bushes, but they were immune to my power. "Saoirse doesn't sense a connection between the waterfall and our spring and neither do I. But..."

"It's too much of a coincidence?"

"Perhaps."

The leaves rustled behind us. I whirled around, my palms glowing, ready to protect my mate. Sledge placed a hand on my shoulder as a dark shape slunk through the bushes.

"Easy, she means no harm."

"She?" I scowled.

"The jaguar shifter. She lives on the other side of the lake. Has since your sister showed up, but she's never ventured on our side. She's always avoided us. I figured she wasn't a threat since she always kept to herself and there's plenty of wild pig around these parts." He shrugged.

I folded my arms. "So why is she here?"

Sledge sighed. "I suppose now I'm Alpha I should ask her."

I rolled my eyes.

Sledge groaned. "You know what your eyerolling does to me."

More leaves rustled as the dark cat bounded away. Sledge stripped and shifted into his wolf and gave chase. I collected his clothes and dashed after him, letting the power of his mating mark pull me in the right direction. By the time we caught up to the big cat, she was on the other side of the lake. Sledge's wolf nose twitched before he shifted. I stepped in front of him and handed him his clothes.

The jaguar hissed and slashed her claws at us.

"Shit, she smells familiar. Like Saoirse did when I first met her." He rubbed his forehead.

"What does that mean?"

"It means she smells like a sister."

My mouth fell open.

"Which one of your brothers is mated to a cat shifter?" Sledge asked.

"No." I shook my head. "Really?" I raised my eyebrows. "Shite."

The jaguar turned away from us.

"Wait! Are you Rian's or Lorcan's mate?" My heart raced at the notion another one of my siblings had a mate here on Earth. Father would have to unlock the veil now. If three of us found mates on Earth, then the rest of the Fae might find theirs. There was hope now for the Fae. A chance they'd have successful pregnancies. Hope they'd be as happy as me with my mate.

If we could fix the spring, then everything would be perfect.

The black cat disappeared into the thick undergrowth.

"But?" I sighed.

"Don't worry, sweetheart, whoever's mate she is, she's family, and we'll protect her too."

I slid my arms around Sledges waist and kissed him sweetly on the lips.

"Fate picked me the perfect mate," I said.

"Right back at you, sweet thing." Sledge winked.

I smiled with so much happiness that I was certain I glowed from head to foot. For Sledge had given me more than a mate, he'd given me hope where there once was none. Hope for my family, for the Fae, for a cure to our dwindling spring of life. Hope was powerful. As powerful as love. Together our love was even more powerful for our future together as fated mates.

FATED MATES OF THE FAE ROYALS

1. Fae's Song

2. Fae's Wolf

3. Fae's Alpha

4. Fae's Heart

5. Fae's Witch

6. Fae's Dream

7. Fae's Fate

8. Fae's Love

Acknowledgments

First, thank you to my family for putting up with me disappearing into the world of books. To Belinda, thank you for encouraging me to write again after I lost everything in a computer crash. Remember to back up! A lot of work goes into creating a story, and I'm always thankful for the support of my online writing buddies, beta readers, and fellow authors, Immy for always making me smile, Tammy for believing in me from the start, Karen for being willing to read any level of heat I write. Cassie for her hand holding. Lana for her invaluable knowledge. Also, my fabulous beta reader Erica and her help with US English. The biggest thank you goes to my 'twin' Dannielle, who is the best critique partner, cheerleader, and sounding board ever, and is forever fixing my comma errors, sorry Dannielle I'm afraid you're stuck with them and me. Finally thank you to all you romance readers. You are my tribe.

ALSO BY

FANTASY AND PARANORMAL ROMANCE
Summer Court

Fae's Song

Fae's Wolf

Fae's Alpha

Fae's Heart

Fae's Witch

Fae's Dream

Fae's Fate

Fae's Love

CONTEMPORARY ROMANCE
Billionaires' Reluctant Brides

Their Love Deal

His Pleasure Contract

Love Negotiations

Her Love Submission

Hollywood Hearts Short Stories

How The Grinch Lusted After Santa

Lusting After Valentine

The Lustful Leprechaun

The Lust Bunny

Lustman To The Rescue

The Lust Giving

Hope Bay

Moving On With Mr. Fix It

Falling For Mr. Faking It

Anthologies

Reluctant Bride

Alpha Male

ABOUT AUTHOR

Helen Walton is a tea drinking, chocoholic, romance writer. Stories are her obsession. She adores creating sensual romances containing a sprinkling of humor and the all-important happy ending. She lives in South Australia with her family, and menagerie of quirky animals where they all take her away from her book world and demand to be fed. Lucky for them, she enjoys cooking but prefers baking.

Sign up for my newsletter for exclusive content.

https://www.helenwaltonauthor.com/newsletter

Visit my website

https://www.helenwaltonauthor.com/

Follow me

bookbub.com/profile/helen-walton

facebook.com/Helen-Walton-Author-1034966677
06602/

goodreads.com/author/show/20249188.Helen_Wa
lton

instagram.com/helen.walton.author

tiktok.com/@helen.walton.author